I0676252

UNICORN KEEP

ANGELIA ALMOS

THOROUGHWEB PRESS

Unicorn Keep

Copyright © 2012 Angelia Almos

Front Cover Design by Melody Simmons of eBookindiecovers.

All rights reserved. This book or any portion thereof may not be reproduced or used in any manner whatsoever without the express written permission of the author or publisher except for the use of brief quotations in critical articles or reviews.

This is a work of fiction. Names, places, businesses, characters and incidents are either the product of the author's imagination or are used in a fictitious manner. Any resemblance to actual persons living or dead, actual events or locales is purely coincidental.

Published by Thoroughweb Press.
P.O. Box 18848
South Lake Tahoe, CA 96151
www.thoroughweb.com

ISBN: 0692327193
ISBN-13: 978-0692327197

ACKNOWLEDGMENTS

Thank you to everyone who encouraged and helped in the creation of this book. To my husband and two daughters who put up with me glued to my computer for a very long time. A big thank you to my wonderful beta readers, Scott Derrick, Jaye Shields, and Denise Stanley. And to my copy editor, Diane Noland. All of your input was crucial in the creation of this book.

A final thank you must go to Ginger, the real pony, who was a part of my life off and on from my teenage years to two years ago when we sadly said goodbye as she went to the Rainbow Bridge. The real Ginger was a spunky and sassy Shetland pony who took many children on rides out in the wilderness and within the safety of an arena. The Ginger in *Unicorn Keep* is modeled off her though I needed to make her a larger Welsh style pony for the sake of the story, but the personality is spot on for the real life Ginger.

CONTENTS

1. UNICORN KEEPER SELECTION

THE MAGES WOULD judge all children between the ages of ten and fifteen at full light. Jiline hesitated outside the village square. Her stomach fluttered as she stayed in the dark corner of the livery stable. The village of Ainsley was not quiet. Voices wrapped around her. Some of the voices belonged to her friends. Any of them could be selected by the mages.

Rain clouds covered the sky. There would be no pretty dawn for the selection.

"Jiline," a voice whispered behind her.

She jumped, so focused on the square, she missed her best friend coming up behind her. "You scared me."

"Sorry," Madelen whispered. "What are you doing?"

"Watching," she whispered back.

Their fingers intertwined as they held hands. Jiline checked her friend over closely. Those in the village joked that the two girls looked more like sisters to each other than to their own siblings which was true. They were both fifteen years, same height, brown hair, green eyes, even the same mouth, but Madelen was the pretty one.

Madelen had been scared when word came out about

the arrival of the mages coming into the village last night. So scared she had cried. She didn't want to be chosen for a life of servitude. Not when the mayor's son was in love with her. The mayor had made an offer for her a few months ago and her parents had accepted. In a little over a year, Madelen and Wilm, the mayor's son, would be wed. Even without the prospects Madelen had Jiline wasn't any more thrilled about the prospect of being drafted by the mages.

Madelen's face showed no sign of the crying Jiline had tried to comfort her through. Her mother must have done something to hide the lack of sleep. Appearances were very important to Madelen's mother.

"I was waiting for you," Jiline whispered.

"You didn't have to."

She smiled. The dark gray was easing to a light gray and the children in the square suddenly hushed. The mages had arrived. Neither of them moved at first. Instead, their eyes locked and they stared at each other. But they had to go. Jiline reluctantly led her best friend around the building to join the small group gathered at the old well.

The three mages stood apart staring at them like insects. Their hoods covered their heads. The mayor stood next to them if a few feet away. Madelen sniffled and Jiline spotted Wilm standing behind him.

"Don't cry," Jiline whispered under her breath as they joined the other children and young people from their village.

Madelen nodded and her lips curved into her brave

smile. Her fingers tightened around Jiline's and she squeezed back.

"All children who haven't reached their tenth year and who have reached their sixteenth year may return home," one of the mages boomed out.

The group jumped and didn't move for a moment, but slowly about half the group dwindled down until there were only twelve. It appeared many of the families hadn't heard the age part of the summons or perhaps they hoped it wouldn't be enforced. She scooted closer to Madelen not liking their odds. How would the mages choose?

As one, the three mages stepped forward. She could now see inside their hoods. Two men and the middle one was a woman. The woman mage stood about a foot in front of the two men and she stared at each of the children in turn.

"I am Mage Daniah," her voice spread over the square. "Your families have a wonderful opportunity presented to them today. One of you may become a Unicorn Keeper."

Jiline's breath stopped. Her parents had been whispering last night as to why the mages had come. Sometimes mages traveled looking for apprentices, but occasionally they needed new keepers: children and young people of pure thought to care for the unicorns which a small group of mages protected year-round at the Keep.

"This is a great honor for your family." Mage Daniah paused and looked down the line again. Her hand suddenly appeared from the swirling robe. "The crystal will tell us if your heart is pure enough for the unicorns. They cannot be fooled. They demand the purest of souls to be in their presence."

Daniah walked to the other end of the line from where Madelen and Jiline stood. It looked like they would be judged last. Daniah held the crystal up right in front of the face of Jonny. The crystal didn't do anything. Of course, she wasn't sure what the crystal was supposed to do. Maybe it talked to the mages. But she couldn't see it doing anything.

Daniah dropped her hand and stepped up to the next child. Her hand came up and the crystal began to glow. Madelen's fingers tightened in her hand.

"What is your name child?" Daniah demanded.

"C-Cris," the ten-year-old girl stammered.

One of the other mages pulled out a parchment. He jotted something down on it. Daniah lowered the crystal and stepped back to say something to her partner. After a brief whispered conversation, she walked up to the next child. No glow. Then the next. No glow. Three more. No glow. The seventh in line. The crystal glowed.

Burrt was fifteen and he didn't stammer when he said his name. "Burrt."

Daniah again confirmed with the other two mages. The last mage had yet to do anything as far as Jiline had seen. Daniah went through the rest of the line until she reached Madelen.

The crystal glowed. Her hand ached from Madelen's iron grip.

"What is your name child?" Daniah demanded when

Madelen didn't offer it right away.

"Madelen," she whispered.

Daniah stepped back. More whispers and writing on the parchment. The crystal did not glow for Jiline. An odd sort of deflation filled her. Her soul wasn't pure enough for the unicorns. She scuffed her foot and looked at the cracked rock under her feet.

"You may go home now," Daniah said loudly. "Those of you who have been chosen inform your parents to come and meet with us today to discuss your selection."

The three mages turned and retreated back to the mayor's house.

Madelen's shoulders shook and she turned to her friend in a panic. "I knew I would be chosen."

"Come on." She tugged her friend back toward the livery stable.

Madelen's feet dragged, but she scuffled after her from Jiline's firm pulling. They would both have to break the news to their families. Jiline should have been relieved over not being chosen. But again the realization that the unicorns found her wanting was depressing.

The old road curved away from the village toward the small woods on the west side. She cut through the grass down a well worn path, a slightly shorter route over the river to both of their family farms just past the river. It wouldn't take them long to get home.

Madelen was quiet with her thoughts as they stepped into the airy woods. The river's gurgle revealed itself several steps before they could see its path among the trees. They had just reached the log which acted as a bridge when Wilm was suddenly upon them.

Madelen dropped her hand as Wilm pulled her into a hug. Jiline instantly felt unwanted as she always did when the two were together. She knew it wasn't out of meanness, but they tended to forget whoever was around them when they were together. It had been like that for almost a year.

"They can't take you," he whispered. "I'll talk with my father."

Madelen nodded her head against his shoulder. Jiline stepped quietly away and crossed the log. She glanced over her shoulder once she was safely on the other side. The two remained in their embrace.

She ran the rest of the way home. Her six brothers and sisters waited for her. It occurred to her that she was the only one of her siblings who had gone. Her younger brother was ten. Why hadn't her parents sent him to the village square this morning?

"Well?" Her eldest sister, Cayla, demanded as she ran into the front yard.

Cayla was yet to be married. Their mother worried her surly personality was keeping away any eligible beaus. With no money to offer, it was up to each of the children to find their own partners or a trade. Cayla had yet to find either even though she was seventeen.

She almost said she wasn't chosen, but something held her back. Instead she shook her head and ran past them to where her mother would be hanging the wash. Why hadn't Kile gone with her?

As she had guessed, Imagene hung the laundry on the other side of the house. Her father, Blake, sat under the tree. They both turned when they heard her. Her father wasn't out working the fields. She hesitated again and shuffled her feet as she came to a stop.

"Were you chosen?" Blake asked, his voice unusually soft.

She shook her head slowly.

"Who was chosen?" Imagene asked.

"Cris, Burrt, and Madelen."

Her mother shared a grown-up look with her husband. "Go get to your chores. Tell your brothers and sisters to finish theirs as well. We haven't been able to get anything done all morning."

She turned to do her mother's bidding and bit her lip before blurting out. "Why didn't Kile come with me this morning?"

Her mother had already turned back to the laundry, but her arms paused in the act of pinning a shirt.

Blake's eyebrows came together in a frown. "Kile is too small."

His tone clearly indicated that was the end of it, but she went on. "They wanted children ten through fifteen."

This time an eyebrow raised at her challenge. "He'll pass as nine. Do as your mother bid."

Chastised, she hurried forward, but something made her hesitate at the corner of the house. Her siblings were still out of sight.

"She wasn't chosen," Imagen's voice drifted to her.

"There's no use dwelling on it," her father said gruffly.

"I had hoped. She has no prospects here, Blake."

"We'll figure something out for her."

"We still haven't found a place for Cayla or Sussy."

"Hinry's sweet on Sussy."

"His parents won't allow him to make an offer. They're hoping it's an infatuation that will fade."

Jiline slowly backed away from their private conversation now that they weren't talking about her. Coming to the front of the house, she stared at her two older sisters. Seventeen and sixteen they should have been married or apprenticed by now, but their village was small. No one offered apprenticeships here because their own children worked their trade. Her older brother, Joshoa, at fifteen had been lucky to find an open apprenticeship two villages over. Her parents were concerned over her own prospects. She was a year or two away from when she should be apprenticing or marrying. There were few boys her age. One had just been selected by the mages. And no tradesmen in the surrounding villages were accepting apprentices from other villages.

Things might be better in a few years for Kile and baby Kait. Kait spotted her and ran over for a hug. She wasn't a baby anymore at five years, but they still called her baby Kait.

"What happened?" Kait asked.

"I wasn't chosen," she said, picking her up for the hug. She leaned her forehead against her sister's. "So I'm staying here."

"Yay!" Kait yelled, wiggling back down to the ground. "She's staying."

Cayla and Sussy nodded slowly. They must already know what Jiline was just beginning to realize. Her parents had wanted her to be chosen.

"We're to get to our chores," she voiced her parents' message.

Kile groaned, but obediently headed toward the fields to meet their father. Jiline walked to the barn, realizing their horse hadn't been hitched to the plow. Three horses munched the hay she had thrown to them on her way to the village. Only one was workable on their farm, really, but the other two worked as she found jobs for them. Night wasn't quite black, but a dark bay gelding who was as old as Cayla. He was an excellent weed eater since he was rope smart and she could tie him anywhere.

Ginger, a pony, was just too small. Father had traded an old wagon for her almost ten years ago to pull their own cart. But they rarely hooked up their cart unless they had something to trade at the market. Once a month was what they averaged during the good months. And Fire, the plow horse, could pull the cart just as easily.

Fire was who she came to pull from the corral. The mare was big and bulky with a sweet disposition. She worked tirelessly despite not getting much help from the rest of her herd. But she didn't seem to care.

"Hey, Fire, girl." Jiline rubbed her copper colored coat as she slipped through the railings.

Grabbing a brush, she quickly got her coat shining as

much as it would before slipping her harness on. Ready to go, Jiline walked Fire out and led her toward where Kile had run off. Her father and Cayla and Kile waited for her. Cayla took hold of Fire to complete the hook up to the plow where her father had left it the night before.

Her job done, she ran back to the barn passing Sussy and Kait in the vegetable garden. She would join her sisters after she finished up her barn chores.

2.   THE PLAN

TAP, TAP, TAP. Jiline peaked out. Her room was dark. Tap, tap, tap. Rolling over, she stared at her window. Tap, tap, tap. Someone was out there. She leaned forward to peer out. A figure was crouched. She couldn't make out who it was in the darkness, but she opened the window without fear.

"Can you come out?"

It was Madelen.

Jiline crawled to the foot of her bed to grab her cloak and shove her feet into her boots. She glanced at her sleeping sisters. Somehow they hadn't heard Madelen's tapping. The room barely held the four small beds. Her father had made them special once Kait was born. She hesitated. Of course, they had probably figured Cayla would have been gone by now and Sussy should have been gone or preparing to leave.

Careful not to get her dirty boots on the blankets, she slipped through the open window. Dropping to the ground, she slowly swung it shut. Madelen reached for her hand and they ran quietly around the house to the barn. The horses were still outside since summer was turning into fall. The nights were pleasantly cool at the moment, but it wouldn't be long before they became cold and the rain and snow would pelt them. For now the horses enjoyed their nights outside. The girls went into one of the large stalls to hide behind the wall and sit on the dry grass currently stored there.

She waited for Madelen to speak. Her friend was the quiet one of the two of them while she had a hard time muzzling in what she was thinking before blurting it out. A flaw which got her in trouble on more than one occasion.

"My parents couldn't persuade them from taking me."

Jiline put her arm around her friend's shoulder. "I'm so sorry. When must you leave?"

Her best friend was about to leave forever, she blinked as her eyes burned with unshed tears. Her stomach hurt at the thought, but she didn't say anything else.

"Soon," Madelen whispered. "They left a letter with directions and a map with my parents. I'm supposed to reach the Keep before the harvest moon otherwise I'll be locked out until spring from the snow."

Madelen would hate being away from her family and Wilm.

She thought about what Wilm had said by the river. "What about the mayor? He couldn't persuade them?"

Madelen shook her head. "Wilm said he refused to speak on my behalf. Afraid of angering the mages." She picked up a strand of grass hay and began to pick the flowers from it, her eyes darted to Jiline's face and away.

She recognized the look. Madelen was holding something back. "What is it?"

"You have to promise not to tell."

"Of course," she whispered.

"Wilm wants me to run away with him when I'm supposed to go to the mages."

She bit her lip, surprised yet not surprised. It sounded like something Wilm would say and do. Her best friend would still be gone, but maybe she would be happy as long as she was with him.

"I told him he was being silly," Madelen whispered, shaking her head. "He doesn't have a trade. I don't have a trade. How would we live without support?"

Trust Madelen to look at the practicalities of the romantic suggestion, but she had a point.

"What did he say?"

"It isn't important. If we had more time, he could go and learn a trade as he planned before we married. But no one in town is accepting apprentices. Not even his father could convince anyone."

"Everyone has their own children to train." It suddenly occurred to her that she had no idea what the mayor did except be mayor. He was the wealthiest man in town, but she didn't know how he came to be.

"The plight of everyone." Madelen leaned against the wall. "So, I go to learn to be a keeper. If I'm lucky perhaps they won't like me and I'll be sent home. Wilm says he'll wait for me."

She leaned forward a little at the possibility. "Sent home?"

"Not everyone who's selected actually becomes a unicorn keeper." Madelen brushed some grass clinging to her skirt. "I'm not sure how. If I did, I could be certain to come home, but some people are sent away in the spring to return home."

"You're smart. You can figure it out," she reassured her, selfishly hoping her friend would find a way.

Tears trickled down Madelen's cheek and she shook her head. "You're the smart one, Jilly, always have been. What if they figured out I was trying to go home? They act like I should be honored, but I'm not and I think she, Mage Daniah, knew how I felt. That was when she told us some children fail the final test and return home in shame."

She grabbed Madelen's hand and squeezed. "It would only be shame if you wanted to be a keeper. You don't want it."

Madelen shivered. "You didn't hear the way she said it. It was a warning to me. I know it was." She wiped at the tears with her other hand. "My parents tried to buy me back. They offered the mages everything, but apparently not enough. Burrt isn't going. I wonder how much his parents gave them to keep him home. Burrt's father couldn't manage the wood cutting business without him."

She hesitated. Burrt had surprised her when the crystal had glowed. "Are you sure they bribed him?" He'd been a mean little boy always picking on the girls and playing pranks. She wouldn't have considered him pure by any standard. "Maybe they realized the crystal made a mistake."

"He's not so bad now." Madelen laughed softly, obviously thinking the same thing.

She shrugged. She figured it was only because he was so busy working with his father. He didn't have time to pull tricks on anyone.

"Wilm told me. Remember the mages are staying in their house. He saw Burrt's father pass a bag to the mages who then said that Burrt wasn't suitable for the task of keeper."

"What about Cris?" She knew the younger girl by sight, but had never formed a friendship with her.

"She's going too, but her parents are excited at the prospect."

Like her own parents. "My parents were hoping I would be selected."

Madelen drew back in surprise. "Why?"

She shook her head not wanting to reveal the details of the personal conversation she had listened in on. "My prospects aren't as good as yours. No beau's waiting in the wings. They'd have to send me pretty far to learn a trade. And here comes a trade offer right to the village."

"Oh, I hadn't realized." Madelen leaned forward to wrap an arm around her to give them both a hug. They held the embrace for a moment. "Funny how you want to go and don't get picked, I don't want to go and do get picked."

Jiline wasn't sure she would say she wanted to go, but she didn't correct her friend's misunderstanding. Madelen started crying again and she hugged her close. Her own heart hurting for her friend's sorrow. It really wasn't fair. How many girls in their village had the prospects Madelen had? None. Here she was no prospects at all stuck in Ainsley a burden to her family.

A completely impractical thought hovered on the edge of her mind. "I wonder how many keepers they select?"

"Hmmm?"

"The Keep. How many days is it away from us?"

Madelen shook her head. "Several days by horseback. Even longer on foot. I can't ride very well so I'll have to walk."

"They don't take you with them?" she asked, wanting to confirm what Madelen had said earlier about the directions.

"The letter, remember, she said because of the sacrifices the families are making they know we need time to get things in order. I don't think that's the reason though."

"What do you think the reason is?"

Madelen shrugged. "Don't know."

She frowned. "Were they returning to the Keep?"

Madelen raised her head. "They didn't say. What are you thinking?"

"I'm just wondering how many villages and cities they visit when looking for keepers." Her idea would hinge on them visiting and seeing a lot of children. "How many of us do you think they see and evaluate? They couldn't remember everyone, right?"

"But they'd know if I didn't come. They have a list of

our names. I saw my name on it. If I ran away with Wilm, what would they do to my family? I think they would do something. Not sending me wasn't an option to them."

"Hmmmm." She couldn't help thinking that if people failed when they got to the Keep that the mages had to select a lot of children to come. How would they know who would pass the final test? Did a lot of them fail or just a few?

"I can only hope they find me wanting in some way. I don't even like horses. You'd think they'd pick someone like you who can ride, train, and do everything with them."

She almost laughed. An ability with animals had not been mentioned as a requirement. "They didn't ask for the best rider, but the purest souls."

Madelen snorted. "You're just as pure as I am. Whatever the heck that means."

"Obviously not."

"You'd probably like it."

"What?" Jiline released the hug and leaned against the wall.

"Being a keeper. Taking care of the...unicorns." She was quiet a moment. "The idea scares me. How do you take care of one? They could kill you so quickly. My parents have a book of creatures with a picture of one."

Jiline nodded, she'd looked through the book several times, fascinated by the color drawings of the marvelous creatures. Many of the animals hadn't been seen in generations.

"Their horn looks very sharp and dangerous."

"It's only for protection, Mady," Jiline reassured her. "You could hardly threaten them."

"You know how you say I need to watch my feet when around my parent's horse?"

Jiline nodded.

"That he might step on it by accident or even on purpose if he gets annoyed with me. What if the unicorns are like that? What if they just stab you by accident? What if they get annoyed at something you do? I don't know a retired keeper. Do you know a keeper? What if they're all killed? That's why the mages have to go so far from the Keep to find more keepers."

Her voice rose with every sentence until she was sobbing again. Jiline put her arm back around her and hugged her close, alarmed by her friend's rising hysterics. She'd never seen her like this. Madelen was the practical, calm one.

The niggling idea at the back of her mind sprang forward. "You don't have to go."

"But—"

"No, you'll go with Wilm." She spoke fast before she could talk herself out of her sudden scheme. "You'll leave for the Keep just as expected. Wilm can head off for his apprenticeship. You two will meet up and go together."

"But they'll know I didn't come."

"No, they won't." She took a deep breath. The plan would not only help her friends, but benefit her family as well. "I'll go in your place."

"The crystal didn't glow for you."

"We'll just have to hope they don't have a giant crystal at the entrance or if they do they'll just assume that I, Madelen, did something between today and then that ruined my soul."

Madelen turned her head to stare directly at her. "You'll go as me?"

"Of course, I can't go as me. My name isn't written on that parchment." She brushed Madelen's hair out of her face with her fingertips. "You know how everyone always jokes we look more alike than different. How we could almost be twins?"

"You're my best friend, if they discovered our deceit..."

"They won't. They won't remember me from today. I'll be you and you'll be me." The plan solidified in her head and became more possible with each passing second. "I'll tell my parents I learned of an apprenticeship for myself. They'll be happy to see me go. Wilm will go to the apprenticeship he's been waiting on. I'll travel with him for safety. You'll go to the Keep. We'll meet on the trail. You become me and go with Wilm."

"I don't know how to do anything," Madelen protested.

She shook her head. "It doesn't matter if there's really an apprenticeship. It's in the city, right?" She vaguely remembered Madelen mentioning his apprenticeship back when Wilm's offer had been finalized.

"Yes."

"So, you'll find a job as a housemaid or nanny."

Madelen raised an eyebrow. As the future wife of the future mayor of their town, housemaid and nanny had not been in her career prospects.

She brought her rushing thoughts to a stop and looked seriously at her friend. "How badly do you want to be with Wilm?"

"You're right." Madelen took a deep breath. "You're thinking too fast for me. Explain your plan one more time."

"IT'S HOPELESS," MADELEN said.

Jiline was supposed to be bedding the horses down for the night before going inside for her farewell dinner. Instead, she was hiding behind the barn trying to salvage their perfect plan. It had all come together better than they had thought it would. Madelen's parents had even insisted she travel partway with her and Wilm for safety reasons.

Wilm paced the length of the barn. "We should have considered how Cris would travel to the Keep. She is only ten and her parents dote on her. Of course, they wouldn't let her travel alone."

Cris' father was going to escort her to the Keep himself and had stopped at Madelen's today to offer to escort Madelen as well.

Jiline chewed on her lip. "Do you think your parents suspect our plan? Maybe that's why they agreed to have you go with Cris and her father instead."

Madelen shrugged. "I don't know. They didn't even ask me if I wanted to go with them."

"Did he say when he plans to leave?"

"Before the Harvest Moon, almost two weeks from now."

"Doesn't give them a lot of time to reach the Keep by the deadline." Jiline considered some way to salvage their plan. "What if we offered to take Cris with us?"

Wilm stopped pacing and turned to where she leaned against a tree across from the barn. "You want to let her in on our plan. She could ruin everything. Expose you to the mages."

"I know, but what other choice do we have?" she asked. "I'm open to suggestions."

Madelen shook her head. "She could never keep a secret that big."

"Madelen's right, we can't ask her to keep such a huge secret," Wilm said softly.

She sagged against the tree. "Suggestions?"

"We need to convince Madelen's parents not to send her with Cris." He walked over to put his arm around her. "What will convince them?"

Madelen took a deep breath and frowned. She was quiet a moment as she thought. "I don't know. But it doesn't matter. We'll leave tomorrow as planned."

Jiline looked over her friend carefully, surprised by her forceful words. "Are you sure? They could try to stop you."

Madelen smiled at Wilm. "They won't get the chance. We'll leave before they rise in the morning."

She didn't think leaving early would really solve the problem of defying Madelen's parents. They must either know or suspect that the three of them were planning something. "And if they come after us?"

"My mother's just as angry at the mages as we are. They won't come after me. I'll leave a note explaining I want my last day with Wilm and my best friend before entering a life of servitude."

3. ON THE ROAD

MADELEN'S PARENTS DIDN'T send anyone after them. Or if they did, whoever it was didn't catch up to them before the trio parted. The road Jiline found herself on was much narrower and not as well traveled as the one which Madelen and Wilm had turned onto. She'd waited at the crossroads until they had ridden out of sight before continuing reluctantly on her journey alone.

She survived her first day and night alone. Well, not totally alone. Ginger, her pony, moved out in an easy stride beneath her. She'd felt guilty when her parents had told her to take the pony to the city and had even given her a little money to help with Ginger's board. She had never deceived her parents before and they had been so happy and relieved. But in a way she was heading off to her new apprenticeship, if a very short lived one.

She expected the mages would discover her fairly quickly. Not that she wasn't Madelen, but that she was *no longer* a pure soul. Once they did, she would head back to the city and meet up with Wilm and Madelen. Madelen would then be safe to return home if she really hated being a housemaid. Wilm could finish his apprenticeship.

What she would do was a little less certain. Returning home without a trade would be humiliating, but perhaps she'd like being a housemaid. She smiled at her own joke.

They should have reached the city by now. Jiline's journey on the other hand was far from over. Ginger, thankfully, was holding up just fine. She patted the mare's slightly sweaty neck. The mountains had been looming over them for the entire day. Night would fall much faster closer to the mountains than in the grasslands where Ainsley was located.

She stopped Ginger at a river crossing and getting off, let the mare drink her fill. Judging the sun's position, she pulled the letter from her saddle bag and scrutinized the directions. Her hair blew across her face and she tucked it behind her ears in irritation. She hated wearing her hair down, but Madelen rarely wore her hair up. So, now she would have to wear her hair down and loose. She didn't mind wearing Madelen's clothes since they were the same size, but the hair thing was going to bother her.

They had tried to make the swap complete by also trading horses, but Ginger had made her point clear when she'd tried to buck Madelen off. Madelen had quickly dismounted and refused to ride her. It added a wrinkle to their trading places plan, but she was glad to have her pony with her. She trusted Ginger as she wouldn't have trusted Madelen's gelding.

She looked at the river and the mountains behind it.

This appeared to be the river on the map. Whoever had drawn the map indicated the river as a good camping spot, but she figured she had a couple more hours of light left and hated to waste them.

It would be at least one more hard day of riding and that would be riding quickly to reach the Keep. Ginger's stride was shorter than a typical horse so it could be even longer.

Ginger's head shot up and she pivoted, her ears pricking forward. Jiline moved quickly and swung onto the back of her pony prepared to meet whatever had caught her attention. Her stomach clenched. What would be worse? Someone sent after Madelen who would know who Jiline was or meeting a complete stranger while alone on the road.

Shoving the letter back into the saddle bag, she fingered the hilt of the blade tucked into her boot. It was more of a multi-purpose blade to cut her food, ropes, or whatever she might need it for. But she'd known when her father had passed it to her as she had prepared to ride off that the main purpose had been for protection.

The bushes quivered and Ginger's body tensed, preparing to bolt away from whatever would emerge. She tightened her legs around the pony's sides to keep her under her.

A boy emerged on foot. A stranger. He stopped, his horse behind him. Ginger relaxed and nickered a welcome. They hadn't seen any other travelers heading for the Keep so far. Jiline didn't release her grip from her knife.

He spoke first. "Greetings. Didn't mean to startle you. I'm Herrick."

She licked her lips and nodded a greeting. "Madelen." The lie didn't come as easily as it should have. She couldn't hesitate in her new identity.

He slowly approached and stopped at the river's bank. His bay horse lowered its head to drink, unconcerned with Ginger's continued nickering.

She released her hold on her knife and patted Ginger's neck. "Hush."

Herrick was still watching her, despite the canteen in his hand, he hadn't made a move to refill it. "You're traveling to the Keep?"

Again she hesitated as she stared at him. Shaggy brown hair, lighter brown eyes, tan, athletic, he looked to be about Wilm's age, but Wilm had been too old to be evaluated. Perhaps he looked older than he was, probably fifteen.

"Yes, are you?"

Herrick nodded. He then crouched down and filled his canteen. She took the moment to study him and his horse. Wealthy. Again like Wilm. This wasn't a farm horse. His tack though dusty was of fine quality as were his riding boots. She shifted in her saddle. She didn't own a pair of riding boots. Just her everyday boots which had been passed down from Cayla to Sussy to her. The clothes she wore were of slightly finer quality since they were Madelen's, but not of the level Wilm or this stranger wore.

He rocked back onto his heels and hooked his canteen to his saddle. His movements were slow, careful. Was he trying to put her at ease? She sat stiffly on Ginger. Her pony had finally relaxed, but she just couldn't dismount even if she looked like an idiot. Of course, his horse could easily overtake Ginger if she tried to run. But Ginger's lack of height would benefit her in the trees and brush.

She would have missed him watching her from the corner of his eyes if she hadn't been so nervous. He futzed some more with his saddle before turning to face her. His horse finished drinking.

He sighed. "We're going the same way to the same place. It would be odd for us to travel separately."

He had a point, but then again, just because he said he was heading for the Keep didn't mean, one, he was trustworthy, or two, that he really was going there.

He turned away to mount his horse. "You're welcome to ride with me or not."

He urged his gelding forward to splash through the river. She suddenly felt completely and utterly ridiculous and let Ginger follow his bay horse. The river was deeper than it looked. He'd picked a path with the least amount of rocks, but being high up his feet were the only thing that got wet.

She wasn't so lucky and quickly scrambled to raise her saddle bags above her head as Ginger sank to almost her own height and pranced across the water. With the splashing, Jiline was truly soaked. She should have waited. She wouldn't dry off before it got dark and it was cold in the mountains at night.

Herrick rode a distance from the river and she

followed him. Settling her saddle bags back down, she considered her predicament. She had one change of clothes which were already dirty. These had been her cleaner clothes.

But wet pants weren't going to cut it. She also didn't want to shove them wet in her saddlebags. If she stayed in the sun as much as possible she might have had some hope of drying them off, but as the trees towered over her she realized it was clearly going to be impossible.

Herrick's horse suddenly stopped and she jerked her gaze from her wet boots to Herrick who was frowning at her.

"Right, pony," he sighed as he dismounted.

Jiline gathered her reins up in worry. What the heck was he doing now? A blanket came out. He held it out to her.

"Once, we hit the trees, the temperature's going to drop considerably. You'll freeze." His words were matter-of-fact.

"I'm aware of that." But she didn't reach for the blanket. "I have a change of clothes."

He lowered the blanket. Shoot. Now she was going to have to change in his vicinity.

"I'll wait," he said, tucking the blanket back into his saddle bag.

She hesitated a second before urging Ginger into a trot to a grove of trees a distance away. Safely enclosed in the circle, she peered out to make sure he hadn't followed. He hadn't even remounted, but leaned against his horse looking back toward the river. She glanced around to make sure no one lurked. Though they would have to be awfully quiet for Ginger not to notice them.

She pulled her dry, if dirty, clothes from one bag and shivered. The damp material seemed to be clinging more than usual with the shade of the grove. Her tunic shirt came off easily and she dried herself with her cloak as well as she could before pulling on the other shirt. Water squished in her boots and she unlaced them. Rolling her eyes, she stepped onto the fallen pine needles with her bare feet. They would dry quicker if her feet weren't in them. Tying the laces together, she hooked her boots to the saddle. She peeked out of the grove again. He was in the same position.

Her pants didn't come off as easily and she had to sit down on the prickly pine needles to finally pull them off her legs. Stepping into her dry pants, she evaluated her saddle. It was just as wet and would make her dry pants soaked as soon as she sat on it.

Her cloak lay on the ground and she had her blanket. What did she need more? Probably her blanket for when they made camp. Folding her cloak, she set it on the saddle. Ginger shook her body and sprayed little droplets on her.

Jiline glared at her, but quickly ran her hands over the pony's coat to push off any remaining water. As dry as she could get the mare, she tied her clothes to the saddle so they would dry.

Ginger shifted and turned to look back at her. She stared at her cute pony in mortification as she realized she looked like a walking clothes line. She was about to untie them to shove them in her saddlebags, but reminded herself to be practical. It would get everything else wet and she needed them to dry before they reached the Keep.

Shoving her pride down and hoping her cheeks weren't as red as they felt, she mounted and rode Ginger out of the grove. Herrick mounted back up without looking at her.

It was only as Ginger reached him that she could have sworn his lips were twitching, but he didn't laugh or say anything. So despite her flaming cheeks she let Ginger fall into step beside him as they hit the well traveled trail into the woods.

Darkness came swifter in the forest as she had expected. She didn't know how she had known that it would, but it didn't slowly gray as it did on the farm, but went from light to murky to dark.

Herrick kept his horse walking for a little while after dark and she had to admit it wasn't completely dark with the harvest moon shining above them, but it made the forest a heck of a lot more creepy. Their ride was conducted mostly in silence. She wasn't sure if he was normally so quiet or if he wasn't talking since she was such a ninny about pretty much anything he did.

At last his horse stopped and Ginger stopped behind him.

"We should make camp here." Herrick pointed to a clearing in the forest just ahead of them.

It was only as she dismounted Ginger that she noticed the fire ring in the middle of the small meadow of grass.

The grass against her bare feet made her feel at home after traveling in the prickly pine needles and dirt for so long.

As before, Herrick was silent as he unsaddled his horse, hobbled him, and then stepped into the woods. She could hear some cracking and breaking, but wasn't sure what he was doing, until he stepped out with an armful of branches of various sizes. He kneeled down at the fire circle and Ginger nickered at the gelding.

Moved out of her stupor, Jiline untied her damp clothes and boots. They weren't quite dry. She would need to hang them up for the night. Hopefully they would be dry in the morning. Looping them over her arm, she shook out her slightly damp cloak. It had done its job of soaking the water up from the saddle. She walked Ginger back to a smaller tree and carefully hung the clothes on its springy branches.

Her saddle and bridle followed. Digging in her saddle bags, she pulled out Ginger's hobble and buckled it around the pony's front legs. A pat on the neck and Ginger walked carefully if slowly toward Herrick's horse. She hoped he was friendly or at least tolerant. Ginger could be a little too social.

With nothing else to do, she did her own slow and careful walk to the small fire Herrick had built, a skill she had yet to master on the trail. Lighting a fire in the stove at home appeared to be a lot less complicated than one on the trail. All she'd been able to do was get some smoke last night.

She felt as if Herrick was staring at her, but he looked

steadily at the flames. She set her belongings down and slowly lowered herself to the ground. The grass had been mostly trampled or cleared right around the fire ring. She glanced around the meadow and wondered at how many people had camped here. How many children her age or younger had stumbled across this small little meadow on their way to the Keep?

"Where are you from, Madelen?" Herrick asked softly.

She jerked her gaze back to him. He was staring at her now. Again, the vulnerability went through her. Which was totally unlike her. She was always the brave one and now she realized how silly it had been to think of herself as brave when she'd been surrounded by things and people she knew.

Forcing herself to breathe when she realized she was holding her breath, she glanced at the fire, before looking back at him. "Ainsley, a small village a few days south of here."

"Your family sent you alone."

Of course they had, they had believed she was traveling on a well-traveled road to the closest city with Wilm as her escort. But she didn't say that. Instead, she sat up taller. "You're traveling alone."

"I'm not a child."

She glared at him. "I'm not a child either."

"You couldn't be more than fifteen."

Her irritation grew at his accurate guess. "Good guess. You can't be much older than I."

He shook his head. "I travel a lot. This journey is

nothing."

Raising an eyebrow at his dismissive tone, she asked him, "Where did you come from?"

"The sea."

She glanced back at the fire. He had traveled a lot farther than she. The sea was at least a week from her village in the opposite direction as the Keep. And the sea stretched on forever according to her father. He'd shown her a map of the coast once. There was more water than land.

"Have you seen the sea?"

She shook her head and wrapped her arms around herself. She watched him dig in his saddle bag and pull out the blanket from before. He held it out and offered it to her.

Embarrassed, she shook her head. "Thank you. I have my own."

Dropping it on his saddle, he watched her again. She was going to have to get used to having the stranger's eyes on her. She didn't know why he made her so jumpy, but it was something she was going to have to get over. He hadn't threatened her in any way and in fact had only offered his assistance. So what if he acted annoyingly know-it-all. He did know how to start a fire. She wasn't sure what time it was, but it was a little early to go to bed.

Biting her lip, she pulled her own saddlebag a little closer and opened one of the bags to pull out the small amount of what was left of the food she had packed. Traveling food was completely uninspiring, she'd been able to eat berries, some greens and fruits while she was in the grasslands and known what she was passing. But the farther away she'd gotten from home the less she had found that she recognized and knew was safe.

She also pulled her blanket out so he would stop offering his own to her. He hadn't spoken again since he'd offered. She really needed to work on her social skills.

Unwrapping the food bundle, she considered the hard biscuits and meat. Yep, very uninspiring. But considering his own generosity, she lowered the bundle so he could see.

"Would you like some? I have soda biscuits and smoked meat, if you're hungry?"

He smiled and slowly shook his head. "I have my own, but thank you."

Setting the bundle in her lap, she chewed on the end of a piece of the salty meat. Though it was probably about an hour away from when she would normally fall asleep, she found it was harder to keep herself erect and her eyes open. Suddenly, all she wanted to do was curl up in a ball.

She slowly wrapped the bundle back up and tucked it away in her saddle bags. She wasn't really full, but no longer hungry anymore. Hopefully she would be able to spot something more appetizing on the trail tomorrow. Of course, she would have to get over her self-consciousness around Herrick. She was going to be around a lot of people she didn't know for possibly the entire winter. She didn't believe it would take them that long to discover her soul wasn't pure, but she wasn't sure.

Herrick flicked his blanket out and lying on his back,

he tucked his hands behind his head. He was now on the other side of the fire and she couldn't see him as clearly. Which meant he couldn't watch her as easily either.

She undid her own blanket and wrapped it around herself before laying down. Using her saddle bags as a pillow, she stared at Herrick's boots.

4. THE KEEP

T HE CHILL OF the morning woke her. The fire pit no
    longer glowed in the gray dawn and Herrick's boots
were no longer where they had been. She jerked up and
glanced around the meadow. He was saddling his horse.
Maybe the chill hadn't wakened her. He finished brushing
grass and dirt off his gelding and swung his saddle up.

Rubbing her eyes, she stretched and slowly rolled to
her feet. Her body was not happy. She'd been so distracted
by her company she'd practically forgotten the soreness
which had begun the second day of her journey. Several
days in the saddle, followed by nights on the ground was
not doing her a lot of good.

Ginger nickered as soon as she saw Jiline up and
slowly ambled over to the camp fire while Jiline gathered
up her things and stomped her feet into her now dry boots
She only had to walk a few steps to meet up with Ginger.
No dirt or grass on her, but she did a visual look over for
any saddle sores. Clear, thankfully. She wasn't sure what she
would do if Ginger developed any. Setting the saddle on

her pony, she was ready shortly after she realized Herrick was watching her again.

Or rather he probably wasn't watching, but was waiting for her to finish. Unstrapping the hobbles, she tucked them into the saddle bags and looked around the clearing until she found the small tree she had left her clothes and cloak hanging on. She was relieved to find them dry, but she glanced quickly at Herrick. He was waiting for her and she hated the idea of changing near him again. Despite the dunk in the river, the clothes in her hand were considerably cleaner than those she wore.

Stifling a groan, she led Ginger behind a large tree on the edge of the meadow away from Herrick. Hiding behind the tree, she changed as quickly as she could, a task considerably easier when her clothes weren't wet. She folded her dirty clothes swiftly before tucking them into her saddle bags.

Checking Ginger's girth, she swung up and bit back the groan as her sore bottom touched down. The soreness would fade to numbness in a little while if her previous days' journey were an example, but the first hour was not going to be a comfortable ride. Ginger walked the few steps to take them around the tree and back into the meadow.

Herrick was mounted and waited on the other end of the meadow. Ginger set forward eagerly to catch up with Herrick's horse before he could leave them. She almost reassured Ginger that they were waiting, but realized Ginger wouldn't be the only one hearing her talk to her horse. Instead, she gave her a pat and a slight sushing noise.

"Ready?" Herrick asked.

She forced a smile. "When you are."

Herrick nodded and turned his horse to head back into the woods. It didn't take long for the serious climbing to begin. Herrick alternated between a walk and a trot depending on how steep the trail was, but she worried about Ginger keeping up and that they hadn't passed any source of water since the river yesterday. She thought of every pound weighing her pony down and was tempted to toss what was left of her food to lighten the load. But the food couldn't even weigh a pound and it would be foolish on her part. Though the letter had made it seem like it was about a day's journey to the Keep, it could be longer.

Herrick suddenly stopped. She pulled Ginger up and tried to look around him and what had caught his attention, but all she could see was his horse and trees.

"What's wrong?"

He was silent a moment. "People."

This time she really leaned to the side to try to see around him. Herrick's horse started walking again. Whoever he had spotted must have spotted him as he raised his hand in a greeting.

"Can we get a ride?" a high pitched voice asked.

Herrick shook his head. "Sorry, they're too tired to carry extra weight. You'll be at the Keep soon."

Jiline still couldn't see who the we was and tightened her hold on Ginger's reins. Three people came into sight a few feet away from her as Herrick's horse passed them. They were glaring at Herrick, but transferred their angry stares to Jiline. Two girls and one boy about her age or maybe a little younger. They had been walking the trail.

One of the girls stepped into her path. "We could take turns riding your pony. It would be the fair thing to do."

Herrick glanced back. "Out of her way, the pony belongs to her."

The girl shot a mulish look over her shoulder at him and didn't clear the trail. Thankful for Ginger's size, Jiline urged her off the trail and around the tree to trot back up behind Herrick's horse. She tried not to, but she couldn't help looking back at them. They had started walking again and were staring angrily at her. She couldn't hear what they were saying, but their mouths were moving.

"They look tired," she said guiltily and forced herself to stop looking at them and to focus on the trail. Walking it had to be awful. She couldn't imagine how long it would have taken her on foot.

"Their journey is almost over."

"How do you know?" She tried to look around him again, but was still obstructed by his horse and the trees.

He glanced over his shoulder and grinned. "Because I'm very familiar with this trail."

She stared at his back as his horse started trotting again. Ginger didn't need any urging to pick up her own pace. He started cantering and then they were both racing up the trail as they broke from the trees. She nearly dropped her reins in shock at the massive stone castle looming over her. It didn't matter since Ginger was completely attached to Herrick's horse and slowed to a stop to stay next to him.

Herrick gestured. "The Keep."

It rose above them. Dwarfing everything around it. She counted four windows above her. She'd seen pictures of buildings that were more than a single story and except for the barns with their hay lofts this was the tallest building she had ever seen in person.

It loomed over her. A giant of stones. It's edges sharp and square.

"Madelen."

She couldn't stop looking at the tower where someone stood on top of it.

"Madelen."

She jerked her gaze to Herrick's.

"The trainees are being gathered on the north side of the Keep." He pointed to where a few other people and horses stood.

She dragged her gaze from them back to Herrick. Herrick who'd ridden the trails before and knew where she was supposed to go. "Are you a keeper?"

He smiled and shook his head. "I'm a mage."

She'd thought at first he just looked older than he was down at the river, but he must be considerably older if he was a mage. Her uneasiness which had plagued her on the trip suddenly gripped her in its hold and she couldn't move.

He dropped his smile as he dismounted. "Good luck with your training, Madelen."

He walked his horse away and she tightened her reins to keep Ginger from following. Ginger danced beneath her and whinnied to her new love. Herrick's horse turned his head and nickered back to her for the first time.

She pulled herself out of her idiotic stupor and fought momentarily with Ginger to go where Herrick had directed her. He had gone in the opposite direction. Five other potential keepers waited with an adult. She frowned at Jiline, but didn't exude the same energy the mages from the village, and now that she wasn't being an idiot, Herrick had exuded. It had to be the power they held inside them.

"Name," the woman asked.

"Madelen of Ainsley," Jiline said, waiting and hoping the woman would pull out one of those crystals.

But she didn't. She just looked over her list and marked it. She glanced over her shoulder and Jiline noticed the open door into the Keep.

"Evie!"

A girl with long blond hair came running and stopped by the older woman who looked to be about her mother's age. "Take Trainee Madelen to the stable and then bring her back to the hall."

"Yes, Mistress."

"Trainee Madelen," she barked.

Jiline straightened her shoulders and suddenly realized she hadn't dismounted Ginger. She quickly did. "Mistress?"

"Keeper Evie will help you with your pony. Do not wander off from her."

Jiline nodded and led Ginger after Evie. She headed in the direction Herrick had gone, wondering if she would run into him again. But the stable was empty except for another young person who was feeding the horses stabled in the large half stone, half wood building built into the side of the Keep.

"We need a stall for Trainee Madelen's horse."

The boy smiled briefly. "Pony, Evie, it's a pony not a horse."

Jiline could see Evie's eyes narrow, but she didn't say anything. The boy waved Jiline over. "I'm Keeper Brody. I take care of the horses. What's your pony's name?"

"G-Ginger," Jiline said surprised by the eager friendliness she saw in his gaze.

Again, none of the uneasiness swamped her as it had on the trail. She really needed to learn to trust her instincts. Not that Herrick had meant her any harm, obviously, but she should have realized that her uneasiness around him wasn't normal.

"I promise to take good care of her," Brody swore.

Evie made a noise and he smiled again.

"They'll be wanting you back quick so I'll go ahead and untack and brush her down if it's all right with you."

She nodded as he expertly plucked the reins from her hand. He passed the saddlebags off to her in the same motion and led Ginger away. Ginger balked for a moment, but followed the boy into a stall. Her ears pricked at Jiline and she nickered.

With Evie's impatient eyes on her, she called, "Be a good girl, Ginger, I'll see you in a little bit."

Evie had already turned and was leaving the stable. She jogged to catch up with her as Evie led her in through another door. They wound through several hallways lit by mage lights. Madelen's parents had given her a book to prepare her for some of the items and magic she would have to become used to. Jiline had done her best to memorize it so she knew that mage lights existed, but she hadn't ever actually seen one and to see the unburning candles glowing was eerie.

A GROUP OF about twenty children around her age gathered in a large room with a giant wooden table which could sit probably double the number of people who were gathered. The three she had passed on the trail were in attendance and not very happy to see her, judging by their glares. Steering clear of them, she sat on the other side of the table and waited with everyone else. Jugs of water and glasses were at each seat. But she hesitated when she didn't see anyone else drinking.

A mage walked in. The robes swirled, but her hood was down revealing her long brown hair. Was it the robes that made all mages look so tall? This woman appeared to be closer in age to the mages who had come to Jiline's village than Herrick.

The mage stopped at the end of the table. "Welcome, new trainees, as you can see we are still expecting more of you, but it is good to see so many of you before the harvest moon ends. Your eagerness speaks volumes. I am Mage Brennah and will be in charge of your training. Full training will launch when all of you have arrived. Until then, those of you who arrived today will be paired up with a keeper.

Your keeper will teach you the rules of the Keep and you will find there are many. The most important is you are not to step outside the Keep without the express permission of a mage. The second most important is you are to do whatever your keeper or any mage commands you to do. We will be testing you this fall and winter. Those who don't pass the test will return home in the spring."

As she spoke, she looked at each of them in turn, her brown eyes settling on Jiline on the word spring. Her stomach clenched. Did Mage Brennah know just by looking at her that she was a fraud?

Mage Brennah's stern face softened into a smile. "Now, you eat."

On that command, several people came in carrying heavy trays overflowing with food and set them on their half of the table. Everyone seemed to hesitate at first, but all it took was one person reaching forward before the table was in motion with people grabbing food and chattering nervously.

The boy she sat next to chewed on an apple and stared openly at her. "Who are you?"

She raised an eyebrow at the rudeness of his voice, but decided he was just as nervous as she was. "Madelen. And you?"

"Billus."

She nodded, but her eyes were drawn to a small group of mages who quietly entered the hall. One was very familiar. Herrick. His gaze rested on her and she dropped her eyes to her lap. He looked like a mage now in his mage robes, but he was considerably younger than the other four who had entered with him. None of them were the three mages who had come to her village. So far so good. Except for the nagging feeling she had that they must know she wasn't Madelen.

5. MAGICAL DRAW

THE FINAL KEEPER trainee had arrived. Herrick watched the father as he kissed and hugged his young daughter. It was unusual for a parent to escort a trainee to the Keep. Not unheard of, but unusual enough to be an irritant to Mistress Marta. She refused the father admittance to the Keep and insisted they say goodbye outside.

Herrick rolled his eyes as he turned away. A trainee keeper hovered just at the entrance of the hall. Madelen's gaze was focused on the open door or the people outside. His stomach flipped as he took in the sight of her. He didn't think she saw him judging by the way she leaned against the doorway, her body hidden from anyone inside the hall.

He had only seen Madelen in passing since leading her up the trail. But he'd developed the habit of searching for her face whenever he passed by the trainees in the hall. They hadn't reached the point where they would be allowed to mingle with the mages or the Keep's guests yet. Still learning the hundreds of rules that kept the Keep operating.

Madelen suddenly darted away. He took a single step to follow her, but paused. He had been doing that on more than one occasion when he caught sight of Madelen. The door creaked behind him. He glanced over his shoulder as Mistress Marta led the new trainee in and shut the door behind her. She paused when she saw Herrick in the hall.

She curtsied. "May I be of assistance, sir?"

He still hadn't gotten used to Marta calling him sir. Didn't matter that he had reached full mage status last winter. He remembered her constant scoldings over the years all too clearly. The small child peeked around Marta to look at him.

He smiled at her. "No, thank you, Mistress Marta. Passing through."

Pivoting on his heel, he headed down the hallway Madelen had sprinted down. He suppressed the urge to quicken his step and glanced in the massive kitchen. She was there with several other trainees helping to prepare the evening meal to serve. He hovered in the doorway, watching.

The head cook noticed him first, but Herrick shook his head before she came over. She sent the trainees out the other door to set up the dining room. He followed behind them walking over to the giant fireplace which was yet to be lit for the evening meal. He could feel the trainees' eyes on his back, but he didn't know if Madelen was one of them secreting glances in his direction.

Someone had laid the kindling and wood within the hearth. It only needed a spark to ignite. Holding one hand below the mantel, he mouthed the fire spell and concentrated on transferring the heat from his body to the kindling. The wood smoked and crackled. The fire sparked to life. A trainee dropped something behind him.

He knew he shouldn't be amused by the reaction but he was. Bracing his hand on the mantel, he angled sideways so he could watch them without blatantly staring. Madelen had her back to him as she picked up whatever she had dropped. By her position, he couldn't be sure if she had even noticed his little burst of magic.

He dropped his gaze back to the fire and watched the flames dance. Why had he wanted her to notice? He'd followed her in here and then flexed his magical muscles to impress her. His eyes moved without thought to follow her movements throughout the room. She was completely oblivious to his presence. Maybe a little too oblivious.

She twisted and pushed her long brown hair over her shoulder, a habit he'd already memorized. Yet, despite her irritation at having her hair in her face, he hadn't seen her tie it back. She leaned over to set a fruit centerpiece in the middle of the table. Her green eyes lifted and met his. Her brows were drawn together. In anger, confusion, he wasn't sure what. They smoothed out as she straightened, a more familiar expression on her face. The same cautious, ready-to-bolt expression she had worn during their journey up the mountain.

He looked away from her this time. He shouldn't be watching her. She was a keeper in training. The rules between mages and unicorn keepers were very clear. No fraternization allowed. The rules of relations with the house keepers were a lot less strident, but he didn't yet know what type of keeper Madelen would be.

Any sort of relations between him and Madelen at this point would be completely inappropriate. It didn't matter, now that he admitted it to himself, how beguiling he found her. He had to stop following her around. The thought solid in his mind, he forced himself to leave the dining room and head toward the main stairs which would take him to the mage level.

He had been following her around. Why hadn't he realized what he was doing? He jogged up the stairs and entered the magic training room. He was normally soothed by the soft light and herbal smells emanating throughout the room, but it didn't do the trick this time. He paced across the room to stare out one of the small windows overlooking the unicorn valley.

The view didn't ease his anxiety either. After a moment, he turned away and moved over to the bookcase. He jerked a well-worn volume out, but didn't open it right away. He had only read the book once before, a study assignment two years ago. The small book contained many variations of love potions. But it wasn't the spells which interested him. He needed to study the section on magical draws and mage courtships.

IT HAD BEEN nearly three weeks since Jiline arrived at the Keep. Not that she was counting the days. Okay, she was, but only because she would have thought someone would have discovered her lack of purity by now. She wasn't popular with the other trainees or the keepers.

Sabrine, one of the three she had passed on the trail, seemed to be making it her mission to alienate her from everyone. It didn't help that they were both assigned to the same dormitory room along with eight other girls. And they all liked Sabrine just fine, but continuously gave her the cold shoulder.

She shouldn't care since she wanted to get kicked out, but she did. The one person who would probably be her friend was the one person she studiously had to avoid. Cris. It had been two days since she had spotted Cris and her father arriving. So far, it had been relatively easy to only see Cris from afar. In completely different age brackets, the only time she was in the same room with Cris was at the evening meal and they sat on opposite ends of the table.

Cris waved whenever she saw her and she did the same. She was fairly certain, Cris believed she was Madelen. Seeing what she expected to see. Thankfully, Burrt's parents had bought his freedom, he would have known instantly she was Jiline not Madelen.

She filed into the dining hall with her group of trainees. All of the groups of trainees were present. The nervous energy in the room was high. It wasn't the evening meal and they were all present in the same room. She tapped her toe on the stone floor softly to try to keep still. With each passing day she was becoming more and more anxious. She couldn't figure out how to flunk out of keeper training. The more mistakes and blunders she made the more tasks they piled on her. She was tired of pretending to be a klutz.

Mage Brennah entered. They all sat up taller. The other five mages, including Herrick, came in behind her. His gaze caught hers instantly and she dropped her eyes to her lap. They hadn't spoken since the day she had arrived, yet he always sought her out. She didn't know why.

She carefully looked anywhere but at him and caught sight of Sabrine poking her friend in the side. The two girls shared a smile and smirked at Jiline. She was sure Sabrine had told everyone about she and Herrick arriving together. She also had a strong feeling that wasn't all Sabrine had said judging by the other trainee reactions when Herrick appeared.

"Today is your first test," Mage Brennah said.

The room instantly became silent. Jiline's stomach twisted.

Mage Brennah's expression was fierce. "And your most dangerous test. We have taught you about the valley the unicorns live in. We have taught you about the Keep. But now you will learn the purpose of the unicorn keepers. You will go down into the valley for the first time and seek out a unicorn."

Her breath caught in her throat as fear seized her. But she wasn't pure. Would the unicorns attack her?

"Now it is up to the unicorns to judge whether you have what it takes to be a keeper. Those of you who pass the test will care for the unicorns as the Keep winters. Those of you who don't pass the test..." She shrugged.

"Some of you may be returning home with the first winter frost."

So this was her way out. She had to fail the unicorn test.

"Be warned, the unicorns can be harsh judges."

She just had to stay alive while she failed.

The mages left the room in a swirl of robes and Mistress Marta entered. The table erupted into nervous chatter as they rose and filed out of the dining room to head down a hallway which had been off limits to them before. Now, the doors stood open.

HERRICK WATCHED MADELEN as she filed out with the rest and suppressed the urge to snatch her. A trainee hadn't been killed in a very long time, but the possibility was there. His feelings for her were growing stronger with each passing day, but were completely inappropriate. His mother paused as she was about to walk by and watched the last of the trainees leave.

"What disturbs you, son?" Brennah asked.

He hesitated in telling her. He had kept his feelings to himself for the first couple of weeks. But he could no longer deny his growing agitation at her being in the training program. He clicked his teeth together.

"Come," Brennah commanded and they followed the trainees path down to the valley.

But they stopped. The mages never went farther than the protection of this overlook. The unicorns might allow the trainees to live, but they would never tolerate the mages inside their sacred domain. Brennah leaned forward on the railing, her gaze following the path of the trainees as they stumbled and slid down the steep trail. Two proven keepers led the way down to the base of the valley.

The unicorns had yet to show themselves. A scrying mirror was of no use. The unicorns' magic blocked any seeing spell. All you would see was fog in the mirror.

He tried to keep Madelen's figure in sight, but she was already heading off on her own. He ground his teeth again.

"Herrick?"

Her tone was clear. She wouldn't tolerate his silence much longer.

"One of the trainees," he hesitated. She nodded her head in encouragement. "I have feelings for her."

Brennah's eyes widened a fraction, before narrowing. "Have you been dallying with a trainee?"

His mother might be the most powerful mage within the Keep, but he still glared at her in spite of the fact that she could send him flying to the valley floor with a single gesture.

"No, I've stayed away from her."

She frowned. "The girl you rode in with?"

He looked back at where he had seen Madelen last and quickly scanned the grassy areas. She had gone into the forest. Stupid girl. She was actually going to hunt out a unicorn instead of waiting like the others. Only a few had ventured into the woods, most moved nervously about the small meadow. They didn't realize and hadn't been told that the majority of the unicorn meadows were past the tree lines.

"Yes."

"What is her name?"

"Madelen." But her name sounded wrong on his lips. It had the moment she had told him, but her gaze had been steady then. Now, she wouldn't meet his gaze.

"She's pretty," his mother said thoughtfully.

He nearly rolled his eyes. There were plenty of pretty girls within the Keep. Many of the male mages dallied with them if they were house keepers instead of unicorn keepers. The mages never told anyone that very few of their recruits actually cared for the valley or the unicorns. The majority of the keepers cared for the mages and the Keep itself. It needed a small army to run efficiently.

He thought he saw her emerge on the other side of the woods, but he couldn't be certain. He didn't realize how much he was straining to see her until his mother put her arm around him.

"You must stop thinking of her."

He sighed, but couldn't tear his gaze away. It had to be her, she was striding bravely through the meadow to another line of trees. Stupid girl. Don't confront the unicorns. "I have tried to put her out of my mind."

"Try harder."

A growl rumbled deep in his chest. "I want her."

His mother's arm loosened and she was quiet a moment. "You feel a draw to her?"

"Yes."

His mother shook her head. "But she is a potential

keeper. A mage cannot be drawn to a keeper in that way. You know this."

"I know. I didn't say it made sense."

"A mage can only be drawn to a mage." She suddenly straightened in alarm. "If she has magic in her, the unicorns will kill her."

His breath stopped. His mother confirming his fears. "She couldn't have any magic in her."

"She must or you wouldn't be drawn to her." Brennah was now scanning the valley as he was, but he knew she had already ducked into another line of trees.

"She wouldn't have passed the crystal test if she had magic in her."

He held on to that. It made more sense for him to be drawn to someone without magic than for the crystal test to have failed. It would only glow when put in contact with someone without a single spark of magic within them. Amazingly most of the population had a little bit even if they never realized it.

It was better for the mages if they never realized it.

His mother uttered an incantation and her hands moved.

"What are you doing?"

"Finding her."

"Your magic won't work." But his words didn't stop her from continuing to try to bring up the image of Madelen in the valley. All they saw was fog in the mirror.

He stared bleakly knowing there was nothing he could do but wait. To go into the valley was unthinkable. The unicorns would seek him out to kill him. His magic would not be able to defend against their attack.

6. UNICORNS

J ILINE SLID DOWN the final few steps of the steep path. The little meadow was crowded with the trainees.

Keeper Kellye cupped her hands together. "The unicorns will seek you out if they approve of you. If you don't see a unicorn we will test you again in the spring. If a unicorn charges you, run for your life. We will be watching."

The two keepers entered the woods in front of her. Somehow she doubted the unicorns were at all tempted to step foot in this crowded clearing so she walked forward to follow the keepers into the woods.

Another giant meadow emerged. A few of the other trainees followed her and they each set their own course through the meadow. She wasn't sure how many other trainees remained in the tiny meadow at the base of the trail. She had to find a unicorn, fail the test, and not get killed in the process. The two keepers had disappeared. There could be even more within the valley watching them, cataloging who the unicorns approached and rejected.

She kept walking without slowing down. The brief glances she had gotten of the valley through the trees as they had come down the trail had shown her it was vast. She didn't know how many unicorns there were or where they were. The unicorns could be on the opposite side of the valley and never even know they were all down here.

She hesitated at another line of trees. They were grouped closer together and let in less light than the previous strip of forest.

"Don't be a ninny goat," she whispered and forced herself to make the first step in to be engulfed by the shadows. The trees surrounded her as she picked her way carefully over downed branches.

A meadow peeked through the trees on the other side of the woods. She quickened her pace to get rid of the rising claustrophobia. A flash of white out of the corner of her eye stopped her dead in her tracks.

Digging her hand against the rough bark of the tree closest to her, she slowly pivoted and looked directly into the eyes of a unicorn. It couldn't have been more than ten feet away. Perfectly still. It's head raised and brown eye focused on her.

The horn glinted in the shadows needing no sunlight to make it shine.

A FLASH OF light from the valley. Herrick gripped the railing tighter waiting for the signal to continue from the keeper.

"Looks like the first unicorn has found a trainee," his

mother said softly.

He had lost track of Madelen. It could be her or she could be in a completely different part of the valley

JILINE TRIED TO remember to breathe. The unicorn stared at her. She stared at the unicorn. Neither of them had moved. She wasn't sure what she should do, but knew she should be worried. Why hadn't the unicorn made a move toward her? It had to sense her unworthiness. If a crystal could, shouldn't the unicorn be able to.

You have magic within you.

The words filled her mind and though the tree she touched beckoned to her with its protection, she couldn't move her feet.

But the unicorn did. Lowering his head, he glided across the forest floor until the sharp point of his horn was inches from her face. She closed her eyes waiting for his judgment.

ANOTHER FLASH FROM the same location, followed by three more. If he could have ripped the railing off he would have. The unicorns were converging on a trainee. It was unheard of for them to converge on anyone but a mage. The magic beckoned and enraged them at the same time. He shoved away from the railing to head for the forbidden trail.

"Where do you think you're going?" His mother demanded.

"You said it yourself. The only way I could be drawn

to her was if she was a mage." He walked into a wall of thin air and spun to glare at his mother.

"They would converge on you just as easily."

"I'm supposed to do nothing. Just let them kill her?"

"They haven't killed a trainee in several generations," she said gently, walking toward him. Her hands moved in a soothing gesture. "Besides there could be several trainees in that slice of woods. We don't know if it is just her."

He sliced the air with his own hand to cut off the incantation she was attempting to weave around him. Slamming his hands against the wall, he attempted to shatter it with a magical blow, but it bounced back. Helplessness filled him. He shook off her hand and bolted for the door that would lead him inside the Keep. There was more than one way to the trailhead.

And slammed into another magical barrier.

THE BLOW DIDN'T come. Her breath was loud in her ears as she waited, but the blow didn't come. She slowly opened her eyes and stumbled back. Four more unicorns stood in front of her just behind the first. Humbled, her legs began to shake and she couldn't draw her gaze away from their deadly beauty. Five horns glinted at her.

You need not be afraid.

The words filled her mind again. Her lips parted, but no words emerged. It couldn't be. Had the unicorn spoken to her?

We will not harm you child. A second voice. Just as strong as the first, but distinctly different flowed through her.

The first unicorn turned his head to glance back at the group behind him. Jiline grappled with what she had heard. Two distinct voices. It wasn't her own mind playing tricks on her at least she didn't think it was her mind.

The other unicorns moved just as suddenly as they appeared. Dancing through the thick forest they were suddenly gone. All accept for the one. His head turned back to her and lowered. The point of his horn was now directly in front of her heart.

Her breath stopped. Time seemed to stop.

He huffed and raised his head back up.

I will not harm you, girl child. You are what we have been waiting for.

SEVERAL FLASHES IN quick succession. Herrick was too distracted to read the code. "What?"

"The unicorns have moved away from the trainee. They weren't converging on her."

"She's still alive."

"It would appear so."

"W-WHAT?" JILINE STAMMERED out.

The unicorn shook his head. *Do not speak. We are not alone.* His body shifted so she now stood beside him looking directly into his eye. *They watch and tell those above what we do.*

A question built, but she bit her lip to keep from speaking. He was talking to her, but how was she supposed to answer him without speaking?

I hear you quite clearly. Speech is unnecessary.

With him standing beside her and the horn pointing away from her, he wasn't quite as intimidating as he had been before. She realized he wasn't the monstrous size she had thought, but was actually dainty and small compared to the farm horses. Not as small as her pony Ginger, but not as large as Night or Fire. No wonder the unicorns had moved so easily through the trees.

Why would you think we were bigger?

The drawings she had seen in Madelen's books had always shown the unicorns dwarfing the people next to them.

He snorted, but no words filled her mind at first. His head raised slightly before his eye focused back on her. *I have lingered with you too long. You must come back to us as soon as you can without the other keepers watching.*

She bit her lip before the words could form again. Why did he want her to return? And she had no idea how she would go about coming down on her own.

Find a way. He shifted and his horn touched lightly atop her head.

He moved just as suddenly and gracefully as the others had and was a blur before he was gone. No longer in his presence, her legs gave out and she sank to her knees and hands on the forest floor. Her arms wouldn't hold her either and her forehead pressed into the mulching leaves. The musky smell filled her nostrils, chasing away the sweet, crisp smell of the unicorn.

"You all right?"

The voice startled her and she jerked up. A keeper knelt down a few feet away from her. She hadn't heard him approach and knew he must have been the one the unicorn had referred to as watching her. Pushing herself back onto her knees, she nodded.

The keeper didn't look convinced. He wore the same clothes the two keepers who had led them down did, brown tunic with brown leather pants, and had a long length of rope wrapped over his shoulder.

"You can go back now. The unicorns chose you as a keeper." He stood up. "Though I've never seen them converge on a keeper the way they did you. I was sure you were done for."

"Me too," she found her words. "Go where?"

He pulled a red scarf from his pocket. "Back to the Keep."

MORE FLASHES FROM different keepers. The unicorns were making themselves known to the trainees. Brennah kept an expert eye on each one. Not knowing what flash might be Madelen, Herrick watched in agony. If he was lucky none of the flashes referred to her. Why he had thought the first flash did, he didn't know. And most likely it didn't.

One of the chosen made her way back into the small meadow. He groaned when he saw the red scarf tied around Madelen's arm. Well, now he knew he wasn't lucky. She was one of the chosen. His mother's gaze shifted from keeping track of the flashes for a moment to look over at her son at his sound.

"She is a keeper. Without magic. And wouldn't be for you."

Knowing that the draw he felt toward her wasn't the magical draw of two mages destined to be together didn't lessen what he felt. Despite what his mother said, he was drawn to her. But if his feelings were true there was more to consider than the protective instincts racing through his blood. The unicorns had not only tolerated someone with magic, but has chosen one to be a keeper.

His mother had taken over the running of the Keep almost ten years ago when he was seven. The unicorns had not been kind to him when he had snuck down there. He knew they had spared his life despite emerging bloodied and with a broken arm. But they hadn't killed him. His mother had raged at him that he was lucky he was a child. Anyone a few years older would not have been as lucky. Madelen was more than a few years older than a seven year old boy.

He walked away from the railing and this time didn't walk into the magical barrier, but tapped it. "Is this necessary any longer?"

He was surprised at her hesitation, but with a flick of her wrist, the barrier dropped and he entered the walls of the Keep.

THE CLIMB UP from the valley floor was way worse than the slide down. The red scarf kept flashing into her vision as she reached forward to scramble up the steep hillside. You couldn't walk up, but had to climb. Sometimes grabbing handholds while other times bracing and scrambling against the steep face. Sweaty and tired, she finally reached the top and was greeted by Mistress Marta.

"Congratulations, Trainee Madelen," Marta said with a smile. "You have passed the first test."

Jiline tugged at her green tunic trying to straighten the dirty material unsure of what she was supposed to say. She had passed the test. Her vision wavered. She wasn't supposed to pass the test. She was supposed to flunk it and be sent home.

An arm went around her waist and guided her into the cool interior of the Keep. She was gently pushed into a chair and she closed her eyes to try to control the dizziness.

"What happened to her?"

The voice was familiar, but her mind was yelling so loudly it barely registered his words.

"She'll be fine. I'm sure she's overwhelmed and tired from the climb. She'll adapt to it in time," Mistress Marta said.

The spots stopped dancing in front of her eyelids and she slowly opened them to see two pairs of shoes standing in front of her. Carefully raising her head, her brain was foggy and didn't quite register that Herrick was Mage Herrick despite his robes. Then it hit her. Mage Herrick. She jumped up and swayed, trying to remember exactly how she was supposed to greet a mage who addressed her.

"Sit," he commanded and stepped forward to nudge her down into the chair. "Get her some water."

Jiline closed her eyes and decided not to worry about

what she was supposed to do. She had a right to be completely and utterly confused not to mention overwhelmed.

His voice was a whisper this time. "The unicorns converged on you."

She peeked at him, uncertain of what he was saying to her. He was right in front of her face, either kneeling or squatting, in a very un-mage like way.

"A death sentence for someone who has magic." His brown eyes were intense. "They let you live this time. They might not be as generous next time."

He rose and took a step back just before Mistress Marta reappeared with a jug of water and a glass. He nodded to Marta and strode from the hallway.

A frown appeared over Marta's eyebrows as she watched Herrick leave before turning her attention to Jiline. "How are you feeling?"

Confused, but she didn't say that. "Better."

Marta poured the glass of water and handed it to her. "Drink this and then return to your room to clean up and change for dinner. Those chosen to be unicorn keepers will meet in the library after dinner."

Marta walked to the entrance of the trail and Jiline guessed another trainee was on their way up.

DINNER WAS UNEVENTFUL except for the hateful gaze of Sabrine focused on the red scarf still tied to her arm. She had forgotten it at first not realizing she had to wear it as part of her uniform. The unicorn keepers in the valley hadn't been wearing red scarves that she had seen. Sabrine didn't have a red scarf on her arm.

Those who did were excused from dinner early and the ten of them filed into the library nervously. She hadn't realized so many of them had been chosen by the unicorns. She wondered if their meet-ups had been as exciting as hers, but she refrained from asking in fear of having to share her own experience.

Mistress Marta waited for all of them to take seats around the library. "Congratulations to all of you for being selected by the unicorns. I hope you realize the great honor which has been bestowed upon you."

She paused as if waiting for them to agree, but no one uttered a sound. Jiline was beginning to realize the mess she was in. She was supposed to have failed the test and be heading home by now.

"You have passed the first test," Marta said. "The first in a line of tests and tasks you will be required to perform to become a unicorn keeper. You will learn about the unicorns, the valley, and what will be required of you in your duty. Unicorn keepers must be fleet of foot, able to climb the tallest tree in the valley, swim the rivers, and run all day long.

"Do not think because the unicorns have chosen you today that they will always accept you. They won't. You must move silently, respectfully through their valley when on duty. You must always be vigilant against the dangers inside and outside the valley. You will study hard and train even harder"

She frowned at all of them as she paused. "Your training starts now. I'll meet all of you outside, in front of the Keep, in five minutes. Be prepared to climb."

7. UNICORN REQUEST

J ILINE STOOD AT the railing and looked down at the valley. As a keeper in training she was allowed here, but not down in the valley yet. How was she supposed to keep her promise to the unicorn? She viewed it as a promise and it itched at her every passing day. It had been four since he had spoken to her.

The real keepers now mingled occasionally with her group of ten. She'd learned there were always five keepers in the valley watching over the unicorns. But she couldn't figure out why they had to watch over the unicorns. The Keep protected the unicorns from those who would capture them and use their magic for evil. But how were the keepers supposed to prevent that from happening. They had no magic to ward off the evil creatures.

She dreamt of them every night, their delicate features and deadly horns, dancing through the forest.

Yet, she never spotted a single one from this balcony. The gate beckoned to her. It was an hour until curfew. There was no way she would be able to make it down and back up in an hour. But she was tempted. Didn't matter that the gate was magically locked to keep out non-keepers. She walked over to it and trailed her fingers down the cool metal. The magic was there. She could sense it, but wasn't sure how.

Someone cleared their throat behind her and she turned expecting another trainee. Instead, Mage Herrick stood before her. She straightened and quickly bowed. Waiting for his instructions, she kept her eyes on the smooth rock of the balcony floor.

"Come here."

She blinked at his strange instructions, but raised her gaze to take the few steps closer to him. He was frowning at her as he had when she'd been chosen by the unicorn. His cryptic message had told her he knew she was a fraud but nothing had happened.

He held his palm up. "Recognize this?"

She glanced at his hand and froze. The crystal. Of course, it probably wasn't *the crystal*, but one just like the one the mages had brought to her village.

"Keeper in training Madelen," his voice was sharp. "Do you recognize this?"

She nodded, unable to form the words. He would know for sure she was a fraud now. But how had he known before?

"The Keep Mages believe in these crystals so completely that it just now occurred to me to wonder why they don't use them when the trainees show up to report for keeper training. Anyone could arrive and say they were someone else. It's a risk. They don't know that the mages who tour the villages aren't the same ones in charge of the Keep or the training. But someone could decide to take the risk. The question would be why."

She couldn't pull her gaze from his eyes. They hadn't left hers the entire time he had spoken. She wondered for the first time what the mages would do to her. Before she had worried about how they would react to Madelen and her family for her not showing up. But now she wondered about her own safety.

He raised an eyebrow. "Why would someone pretend to be a chosen trainee, Madelen?"

She was tempted to confess, but no words came to her. Her promise to the unicorn forced all words out of her mouth. She must return to the valley floor. She shook her head. "I don't know, Mage Herrick."

His frown deepened and he suspended the crystal inches from her face.

It began to glow. Surprise flowed through her and mirrored the surprise she could see on his face. His hand slowly lowered and he tucked the crystal into his pocket. The confidence he had shown a moment before was gone and his frown was uncertain now.

"I bid you good night, Madelen." He didn't wait for her response, but pivoted on his heel and strode back into the Keep.

She stayed out there until curfew and returned to her room just as Marta was about to close the door. She received a frown but no scolding and quickly slipped into bed still dressed but without her boots. No time to change. Her punishment for being late.

A few hours later, she was wide awake and uncertain what had roused her. Sliding carefully from her covers, she picked up her boots and tip-toed to the door. She opened it just enough to squeeze through.

She didn't put her boots on until she reached the gateway to the trail down to the valley. The gate opened as silently as the door to her room had. The mage candles glowed on the walls down the short stairwell to the rocky hillside. The valley was full of shadows. She wrapped her arms around herself at the chill. Winter was coming shortly. None of the trainees had failed the test enough to be sent home before winter. Marta had explained that once winter came no one would leave the Keep and no one would be able to get to the Keep.

The trail looked even more dangerous in the soft moonlight. She fingered the red scarf before untying it and shoving it into her pocket. It was possible one of the five keepers was watching the trail. She tied her hair back and tucked it into her tunic, and was disguised as best she could considering she hadn't thought to grab her cloak with its hood. Already committed it seemed too late to venture back to her room to get it.

She could handle a little cold. Stepping out of the safety of the Keep walls, she kept her head down and went down the hillside as quietly as she could. A challenge she didn't think she managed very well. Perhaps she should have tried for speed. And perhaps she would have tripped and tumbled the rest of the way down.

At least she was now on the valley floor and she sprinted to the first line of trees. Knowing a keeper could be anywhere, she kept her face down and moved as quietly to the next meadow as she could. If the keepers stayed near the unicorns to protect them they would most assuredly spot her if she got close to them. So how was she supposed to find the unicorn without getting spotted?

A flash of white to her left caught her attention. A horn glittered in the woods across the meadow. Taking a deep breath, she didn't allow herself to hesitate, but ran through the second meadow to where she had seen the glitter. The unicorn wasn't there. She hesitated again, leaning against a tree to catch her breath.

A second flash of white deeper in the forest. Holding on to her courage, she weaved her way through the trees going deeper into the woods. This section wasn't like the others. It didn't lead into a third meadow but became thicker with trees.

The flash of white no longer moved and the horn shone in a ray of moonlight. A unicorn stood next to an ancient tree. She wasn't sure if the unicorn was the same one who had spoken to her or one of the other four who had allowed her to see them. A second unicorn emerged from around the wide tree.

She stared at them uncertain of what to do. Was one of them the unicorn she had made the promise to?

You are late.

She thought of Herrick and the crystal.

The unicorn colt raised his head. *They tested her again. Why?*

She shrugged, unsure herself why Herrick had suspected she wasn't pure.

The unicorn colt snorted. *Did he say anything to you?*

She struggled with how to tell them what Herrick had said.

You may speak. The others are distracting the keepers away from us.

She bit her lip before whispering. "He asked me why anyone would want to switch places with a chosen candidate knowing the risk of discovery."

Why did you switch places?

Thoughts of Madelen and Wilm quickly filled her as well as her own parents' worry for their children's prospects.

The unicorn colt stepped closer to her. *She is the one.*

You cannot be sure. It is a great risk we would ask of her.

He raised his head. *You wish to remain in this prison forever? We do not know if another will come who can help us.*

Her eyes darted back and forth between the two unicorns as it occurred to her that she was listening to two unicorns arguing.

The second unicorn gazed at her with deep brown chocolate eyes. *Would you help us?*

Yes, vibrated inside her, but she couldn't fathom how she would be able to help a creature as magnificent or powerful as a unicorn. The magic flowed from every pore of their bodies.

"How would I help you?"

The unicorn colt spun in a flash. *A keeper approaches. You must return to the Keep before you are spotted.*

You take her. I will distract him. The second unicorn flitted through the woods and disappeared.

Come. The unicorn colt commanded.

Jiline obeyed without thought, running after the dancing unicorn back toward the Keep. He stopped at the final line of trees.

Return tomorrow night and I shall explain. Climb quickly, Jiline.

The unicorn colt was gone. Heeding his command, she ran across the small meadow and climbed as fast as she could, scrambling up the rock face. She was sure someone probably waited at the Keep entrance to catch her. But no one waited for her.

HERRICK FUMED IN the library. Madelen was out training in front of the Keep. Marta had them running sprints. Dark circles under Madelen's eyes told him she hadn't slept through the night. He wondered if thoughts of him had kept her up or thoughts of a more nefarious purpose. He hadn't told his mother of his embarrassing attempt to prove Madelen had magic within her.

Yet, she beckoned to him whenever she was near. He could feel her presence before he saw her in a room. It didn't make sense. The book he had been studying on courtship rituals of the mages hadn't been any help. No mention of a mage feeling the draw to a non-magic. Not even the possibility. So, how could he feel it if she had no magic?

"Herrick," his mother's voice was filled with irritation.

He stood up quickly and bowed his head to her as mistress of the Keep even if she hadn't used his title name, her voice certainly put her in that realm. He tried to block the book with his body, but her sharp eyes had already caught what it was judging by the frown on her face.

"This is getting ridiculous," she said sharply. "You are not a child anymore."

He raised an eyebrow at the scolding she was giving him like he was a child, but he didn't voice it.

"You are a young, healthy man, it is perfectly natural for you to be attracted to young healthy girls. It is not a draw that you feel." His mother's voice no longer held it's perfect cadence as she appeared to stumble over her words. "She's a keeper in training. You must leave her alone. A hint of magic on her could ruin her to the unicorns."

"You think I would put her in danger?" he asked sharply.

She hesitated. "There are plenty of other pretty girls here. If none of them suit you, perhaps you should travel again."

He gritted his teeth. He had no interest in heading out on another journey. She'd sent him off to every available young mage woman over the summer in the hopes that he would be drawn to one of them. It hadn't worked. But he had to be careful with what he said. As the Keep Mage it was completely within her right to send him away as a mother could not send her son away. He would have no choice but to obey her if she commanded him.

He kept his eyes steady on hers. "You're right. I was just trying to understand how a draw would feel."

She stepped forward to pick up the book. "You understand the difference now?"

He nodded.

"You're young, you'll feel the difference between regular attraction and a draw soon enough," she said hurriedly.

He kept himself from rolling his eyes. He might not be the most experienced, but he was old enough to have felt a regular attraction for a female mage and non-mage alike. An awkward silence settled between them.

"Well." Brennah smiled. "Times like this make me wish your father wasn't a traveling mage."

He didn't agree, but nodded anyway, anything to get the conversation over. He doubted his father would have been any help at all since they barely knew each other.

HER BODY ACHED by the time her head hit the pillow at lights out. What made it worse was knowing she wouldn't be getting any more sleep than she had the night before. She couldn't allow herself to close her eyes as she wasn't sure she would wake up. Making herself count to two hundred, she peered around the room and listened to the breathing.

She could just make out the shapes of the other nine beds. With her bed against the farthest wall from the door, she would have to pass all of them, five on one side and four on the other to get out of the room. Uncertain if everyone was really asleep inside or outside her room, she made herself count to five hundred.

Silent as she could be, she grabbed her cloak this time along with her boots before sneaking out of the room. She moved with more assurance, but kept her ears open to make sure she didn't run in to anyone as she exited the Keep. The unicorn colt had assured her they would keep the keepers distracted so she didn't hesitate as she swirled her cloak on and descended down the hillside. It wasn't as difficult tonight.

Breaking into a run, she headed toward the third wood she had been led to the night before. A glint of white told her she was heading in the right direction. This time three unicorns waited for her at the ancient tree.

She stumbled to a stop and tried to catch her breath as she waited. None of them spoke right away.

"I'm here."

We see that. The new unicorn said. They all had distinctive voices. *She doesn't have enough power.*

I've hidden it.

The new unicorn stared at the unicorn colt, who looked away.

You sure she can break the barrier.

The unicorn colt raised his head back up. *Yes.*

The new unicorn nodded his head slightly. *Very well.*

With a swirl, the new unicorn flitted through the woods and was gone. Leaving the two original unicorns with her.

"Break what barrier?"

The help I referred to last night.

"Oh." That didn't really explain anything to her. "What did you hide?"

Your magic from the mages. It was how the crystal didn't pick it up.

"Why does it glow if it doesn't pick up magic?" She would think it would glow if it sensed magic.

They did originally. The mages changed it's chemistry to make it appear the crystal is choosing someone when it is actually eliminating who they don't want coming to the Keep.

"But they have magic."

The older unicorn took over explaining. *Most of you do. Very few people are born without a spark of magic. Your mages have learned to grow the spark.*

The unicorn colt snorted. *Steal is more like it.*

They grew their spark to become powerful enough to imprison us and steal our magic.

"Imprison? But I thought the Keep was built to protect you?"

The unicorn mare stepped closer to Jiline so she could look in her eye. *A lie. The valley is our prison. They use our own magic to keep us within the mountain walls. We cannot break them. The more we push at it the stronger it gets.*

Jiline gazed at the mare in horror as images of the unicorns' confinement for nearly two hundred years flowed through her. "I'm sorry."

You are not responsible, Jiline. My son seems to feel you can help us break the barrier.

"But how?" If the unicorns with all of their magic couldn't break a magical barrier, how was she supposed to?

The barrier is tied to us. A human mage can break it. The unicorn colt said. *There is a spot where the barrier is weak. A trail the mages don't know of. The barrier is strongest where we can physically leave and weaker where nothing can actually climb from the valley.*

"The Keep?"

The unicorn colt shook his head. *The Keep itself is a physical barrier. We could attempt to climb the cliff and go through the castle, but they would erect a magical barrier before we could.*

"I still don't know how I'm supposed to help you." And she wanted to help them. The tears still gathered in her eyes from the unicorns' sorrow the mare had allowed her to feel.

You will break the barrier for us.

"But I'm not—"

The mare spoke again. *No, you are not a mage yet, but with our help you can become one. It will take some time. But what is a few months after hundreds of years of waiting. The danger will be to you. If the mages discover what we are doing they will kill you.*

Jiline shook her head trying to wrap her mind around everything she was learning. The killing part didn't really register, it was the becoming a mage that she found hard to believe.

The choice must be yours.

The unicorn colt snorted in protest. The mare swung her horn at him.

The choice is hers. You will not compel her. The mare swung her head back toward Jiline and blew softly over her face. *The choice is yours. We will not force you or harm you if you choose to remain a keeper the rest of your life. Think until the quarter moon. Return then if you will help us.*

8. CHOICES

H ERRICK HID IN the alcove and watched the trainees file
by. The large group split into two. He examined
Madelen as she walked by. Dark circles under her eyes. He
had no interest in attracting her or any of the trainees
attention. His mother was right. He was pathetic. Madelen
had passed the test. She was a non-magic. Yet, he still felt
the draw. He scuffed his boots on the old stone floor once
they had passed him and emerged into the hallway.

He couldn't explain what he felt toward her. The
protective instincts when she went down into the valley had
been more than casual interest as his mother insisted. He
needed to put her out of his mind. It wasn't like he had
nothing to do but follow her around like a little puppy. He
had his own training to see to.

The mage level was at the top of the Keep and boasted
several full windows that looked out over the valley. Not
that it did them much good beyond the view. A flash of
white here or there. The unicorns were not happy. As far as
Herrick could tell, they were never happy.

The keepers were having to stay on their toes to prevent any mishaps. He knocked sharply on his tutor's door and waited.

"Enter!" a voice boomed out.

Herrick heeded his command and pushed the door open. Mage Lionel's blue eyes were steady on Herrick as he entered.

"I leave in a week's time if you would like to accompany me," Lionel said, setting out the workings of a complicated potion for Herrick to mix and execute.

Herrick met Lionel's gaze. His mother at work again? "My mother's command?"

Lionel didn't look away, but his smile turned to a frown. "I spoke with your mother this morning and she felt it would be beneficial for you to not be confined to the Keep all winter. There is plenty of the world for you still to see, Herrick."

"I know there is." He carefully kept his emotions concealed. Something he had learned to do very early on and normally didn't worry so much about. "I'm honored by your invitation to join you, Mage Lionel, but I plan on remaining at the Keep."

Lionel nodded. "It is your choice, but the invitation is open should you change your mind."

Herrick ground his teeth in irritation before stepping up to the table to identify the spell Lionel had laid out for him. He cataloged the ingredients, but his focus wasn't really on his task and he turned back to Lionel.

"Mage Brennah need not worry over me."

"She's a mother. Mother's worry."

Herrick narrowed his eyes and wondered just how much she had confided in Lionel. He knew their relationship had progressed past colleagues while he was gone for the summer. The difference in the way they looked at each other had been clear to him.

"Have you ever felt a draw, Lionel?"

Lionel frowned and dropped his gaze first. "No, Mage Herrick, I haven't."

He was surprised by Lionel's answer. The man was easily forty years. Probably older. "My mother seems to think every mage has a match and will have a draw if only exposed to each other."

Lionel shrugged. "You can love another without a draw influencing you. Personally, I've never wanted a draw. I prefer to be the master of my own fate. The draw gives another person too much influence over your destiny."

JILINE RUBBED HER eyes. The hand-drawn pictures in the book in front of her were beginning to blur. It was several hours after dinner and her group was studying late, again. She closed her eyes a moment and then forced them open to look at the picture of a unicorn battling some sort of dog creature.

They studied the lore of the unicorns in the evening. Well, the unicorns and the creatures who would harm them if the opportunity arose. The unicorn keepers had to be able to recognize the creatures themselves as well as the signs of when one of them was near. She hadn't realized how many other animals and beings the Keep protected the unicorns from. Of course, the unicorns didn't feel that way.

Mistress Marta cleared her throat. "It is getting late. All of you are excused to sleep. We have another long day tomorrow."

Jiline closed the book and carefully shelved it in its place. She turned to leave, but stopped at the moon chart hanging on the wall and frowned. Three days. The quarter moon would rise in three days and she needed to give the unicorns her answer then.

"Madelen."

Jiline jumped and turned. Mistress Marta waited in the doorway. All of the other unicorn keeper trainees had left. She hurried forward and bowed her head as she passed. She walked back to her room alone, but the room was full of many girls. None of the other girls seemed to notice her entering. Keeping her head down, she straight-lined it to her bed against the wall.

Sabrine bumped her as she passed the girl's bed. Jiline was pretty sure she had tried to trip her, but missed. The crabby girl's antagonism had risen steadily in the last couple of days. She gritted her teeth to keep herself from demanding Sabrine tell her what her problem was. It was getting more and more difficult to ignore Sabrine and her little tricks. But she didn't want to draw any extra attention to herself. She got ready for bed as quickly as she could and slipped under her blanket just as the mage lights blinked off.

In the dark, she stared at the ceiling, willing herself to

go to sleep. The room was silent. She should have been able to fall asleep. She was exhausted, but her head wouldn't stop spinning with the unicorns and the decision she had to make in three days. Unable to silence the thoughts, she tossed her blanket back and sneaked out of her room despite not needing to go down to the unicorns.

Instead, she headed for the stable. She didn't have an answer for the unicorns and worried a few days wouldn't give her any more clarity than she already felt. The stable was quiet. The rows of stalls stretched out before her. Brody had brought Ginger outside a few times when they had been training in front of the Keep for Jiline to say hello, but she hadn't been inside the barn since she arrived.

She walked down the long building peering into each stall where a horse didn't already look out. She had been quiet when she entered and most appeared to be sleeping.

At last she found Ginger about halfway down and clucked softly to her pony before letting herself in. Ginger nickered sleepily at her and waddled closer. The mare was starting to get fat. Too much good food and not enough exercise. She glanced around the stable. The majority of the horses seemed to fit that description. How many of the horses belonged to trainees and keepers? They never had a moment to ride or do anything but train or work as far as she had seen.

The keepers who hadn't passed the valley test were all still here. She scratched Ginger under her chin. Why hadn't they been sent home? They had failed the test. Narrowing her eyes, she knew the answer. They were being trained to keep the Keep in motion. It had to be cleaned, food prepared, rooms for the guests made, even Brody had come as a trainee from the few words they had shared.

Her eyes weighed heavily on her and she kissed Ginger on her nose before hurrying back to the dorm room. She fell into a deep slumber until the bell rung first thing in the morning.

Another day of physical training followed with her least favorite activity, climbing. She hadn't caught up on her sleep and knew she was dragging. It didn't help that she kept catching flashes of Herrick watching, distracting her away from the ropes.

She hated climbing. Trees were bad enough, but to climb hand over hand up a rope deep into a tree was impossible for her. Mistress Marta clucked, disappointed in her attempts and excused her back to climbing the two trees which had branches low enough to jump up and grab.

She fared a little better and was able to at least get more than a few feet off the ground. They took their lunch outside underneath the torture devices before continuing to climb the rest of the afternoon. Jiline's body ached and where it didn't ache it was numb. Her hands had reached a point of numbness where she couldn't feel the blisters and cuts covering them.

SHE WAITED AN hour past lights out before slipping out again. She thought about visiting Ginger, but instead went to the library. She wasn't sure what she was looking for exactly, but she had more questions than answers. The unicorns had told her they had been imprisoned by the mages about two hundred years ago.

None of the volumes in the library she had seen were that old. Trailing her finger down the books, she stopped at a stack of scrolls and picked one up and unwound it revealing a drawing of a suitably disgusting creature with four arms, sharp teeth, and one eye, one of the many she was supposed to watch out for as a keeper. Did the unicorns not know or had they forgotten about all the beings who were still trying to get at them because it had been two hundred years?

What if she helped them and the monsters took down the unicorns to steal their magic? Everyone wanted the unicorn magic, even the honored guests who visited here. They came to the Keep because the spells the mages cast here were more potent and powerful than anywhere else. It had to be the unicorn's magic which influenced it.

She went back to her room uncertain of what she had hoped to find, but she returned to the library the following night after lights out. A decision had to be made. She would need to return to the unicorns' valley tomorrow night to tell them.

She stepped carefully around the quiet room. Her feet had blisters on them to match the ones on her hands, from running all day today, climbing the day before, but that was the life of a unicorn keeper according to Mistress Marta. Jiline was thinking it really wasn't much fun despite the honor. She walked directly to the scrolls she had discovered last night. Pulling several out, she sat at a table and began to study them. If only one of them contained the information she needed to make her decision.

THE QUARTER MOON was high in the clear night sky. It illuminated the path down to the valley enough for her to not trip over a giant boulder. She carefully picked her way down. She didn't allow herself to pause when she reached the valley floor, but raced toward the first strip of trees. Hopefully, the unicorns were expecting her and were distracting the keepers away from where she was.

Even with the hood of her cloak pulled over her head, she worried over someone spotting and recognizing her. Now that she knew the techniques of the keepers she didn't pause at the edge of the first strip of trees. Keepers kept to the trees. Better to stay moving. She curved left when she reached the second meadow going toward where she had met the unicorns before.

A flash of white let her know she was going in the right direction. Keeping her face tilted down, she met the two unicorns next to the ancient tree.

Their voices didn't fill her head as they had before and she bit her lip and looked from the unicorn colt to the unicorn mare.

"I want to help."

I told you she would say yes. The unicorn colt was almost gleeful.

You must be sure, Jiline of Ainsley. The unicorn mare said with caution. *You will have to leave everything you know behind if you assist us. The mages will strike back against whoever helps us.*

You can't stay here, but will need to leave with us.

She hadn't considered leaving with the unicorns when they escaped, but she supposed helping them was one way to fail at being a keeper. She took a deep breath.

"How do I help?"

The unicorn colt stepped closer. *You'll break the barrier for us.*

Her momentary burst of confidence quickly deflated. They expected her to break the magical barrier surrounding the valley.

Not break, exactly. The unicorn mare said.

"But how can I?"

The magic is within you.

They had mentioned this magic to her before, but she still had a hard time believing that even if she had magic within her that it was enough to take down something as massive as the barrier.

The unicorn colt tossed his head. *Do not doubt yourself, Jiline. I know you can do it.*

Both of the unicorns pivoted suddenly, their ears pricked forward. The unicorn colt turned his head back toward her.

A keeper approaches quickly. You must return to the Keep before he spots you.

9. FALSELY ACCUSED

OBEYING THE UNICORN colt's command, Jiline sprinted back through the woods and meadows to the trail. She scrambled up, worried she wasn't quick enough. It would be just her luck to be caught now. But no shouts rang out. Ducking inside the gate, she stopped and leaning forward, her hands braced against her knees, attempted to catch her breath.

Only a few mage lights flickered, barely illuminating the hallway. Not that she needed the illumination. She had snuck around enough in the shadowy darkness to know her way back to her room with her eyes closed. Her breathing finally evened out and she headed quietly back down the hall toward the dormitory rooms. She had to be especially careful as she passed the entrance to the main hall. But all was quiet.

"I knew it," a voice said behind her.

She spun. Not as quiet as she had thought. Sabrine stood in the hallway just behind her. She had no idea where the girl had come from.

"Sabrine," she said, trying to think of something to say. She looked past her for anyone else who might be with her.

"I know you sneak out to visit him," Sabrine snarled. "You should be ashamed of yourself. Defiling yourself in that way. You were chosen to be a keeper." She pushed her shoulder and stalked past. "And yet you go to Herrick nightly."

Jiline froze in panic before running after Sabrine to grab her arm and stop her.

"Don't touch me, you're disgusting," Sabrine said. "I'm telling Mistress Marta and she'll kick you out as you deserve. You might have them fooled, but I've always seen right through you."

"Sabrine, it isn't what you think." She hunted quickly for a lie and spotted the library door. "I've been studying. Being a unicorn keeper isn't as easy as you seem to think it is."

Sabrine shook her head. "Do you think I'm stupid? We all see the way Herrick watches you." She sniffed loudly. "It's perverted."

"I can't help that." She had no idea what Sabrine was talking about. Yes, she noticed Herrick watching her when she couldn't avoid him, but he was frowning in suspicion not leering in lust. "Besides, he watches everyone." Didn't he?

"No." Sabrine crossed her arms. "He only has eyes for you."

She blinked at the jealous tone in Sabrine's voice. "You like him, don't you?"

Sabrine stepped back, her eyes flitting away from Jiline. "No!"

"You do." She grabbed onto the feeling with certainty. "Did you offer yourself to him and he rejected you?"

She had seen a girl house keeper flirting with one of the male mages. It didn't take a genius to know what they had gone to do when they had slipped out of sight. Sabrine spun back around to march down the hallway.

Herrick stepped into Sabrine's path. "It's long past curfew."

Sabrine shot a triumphant look at her and grinned. Great, there was nothing she could say which would dissuade the girl now. Despite Sabrine's sharp tongue with her, all she did was curtsy quickly to Herrick and run back toward the dormitory. Jiline should have been as quick, because she found herself alone with the one person who suspected the magic the unicorns had hidden within her. Their warning of what the mages would do should they discover her deceit rang loudly in her head.

Herrick's eyes narrowed and he stepped back. "You shouldn't be wandering the halls at night."

Her tongue felt heavy in her mouth. "Of course, I apologize, Mage Herrick." She bowed her head formally and stepped back quickly to follow Sabrine's path.

"What were you doing?"

She paused. "I like to study in the library when it is quiet." What if he had just come from the library? "And visit my pony. There's no time in the day."

"You need sleep more." He turned and walked away

from her toward the main hall.

Stunned by his sharp words, she waited a full second before running back to the dormitory. Sabrine was already back in her bed and pretending to be asleep. Jiline tiptoed past her and slid into her own bed.

Mistress Marta separated her from her group shortly after breakfast. They climbed the stairs to the mage level. Jiline's heart began to race and she sweated. She hoped this was about Sabrine's lie. She had seen the girl talking with Marta just before breakfast, but had dared to hope it was about something else when Marta hadn't looked at her. Now, she wished it was about Sabrine's lie as the only other alternative was they had discovered where she had really gone last night.

Twisting her fingers together, she stood next to Marta as she knocked on a heavy wood door.

"Enter," Mage Brennah's voice rang out.

She closed her eyes in despair. What could it be but the unicorns for her to be summoned by the Keep Mage? Marta opened the door and not too gently pushed Jiline in over the threshold before shutting the door.

Mage Brennah sat behind a large wooden table covered with what Jiline could only assume was magical items since very few of them looked familiar to her. Brennah rose from her seat and walked slowly around the table.

"Do you know why you have been summoned, Trainee Madelen?" Brennah's voice held an odd note to it and Jiline reluctantly stepped forward.

She shook her head, but her mouth wouldn't move. Something tugged inside her.

Brennah frowned at her lack of response. "Confession is good for the soul."

Terror froze her in place. They knew about the unicorns. But maybe not. Just as with her parents when she had done something wrong it was better to admit to as little as possible. Asking for a confession was a trick adults used to get you to admit what they might only suspect.

Brennah's lips pressed together for a moment, before she turned and returned to her chair behind the table. "Sit."

Jiline forced her legs forward to sit in the high-backed chair positioned on the other side of the table.

Brennah was silent a moment as she stared at her. "Being a keeper is a great honor, would you not agree, Trainee Madelen?"

She bobbed her head. "Y-yes."

"Yet, you would risk this opportunity we have given you."

"I don't understand." Better to play dumb than to admit to anything.

"Breaking curfew is a serious infraction. The rules are in place for a reason. Mistress Marta had noticed your lack of drive and energy the last few days. Perhaps contributed by your evening strolls."

Admit the truth when you knew they knew. She glanced down at her twisting fingers and forced them to be still. "I haven't been able to sleep."

"And why is that?"

She shrugged. Maybe Brennah didn't know about the unicorns. You could hardly call climbing down to the valley a stroll. "The task of unicorn keeper overwhelms me. I was trying to understand better and thought if I studied extra I wouldn't be so nervous."

"You've been studying?"

"Yes, ma'am." Jiline nodded.

Brennah sighed. "Lying won't help you now. I know what you have been doing. Perhaps, you didn't realize that a keeper not only has to be pure of the soul, which telling lies corrupts, but pure of the body. Having physical relationships with another is strictly forbidden."

This was about Sabrine's lies. "I'm not lying."

"Where were you last night, Trainee Madelen?"

"I went to bed, but couldn't sleep. I walked around and studied the unicorn tapestries in the hallways. There are many within the Keep." It would be easy for someone to walk the many hallways and not run into another soul.

Brennah slapped her hand down on the table and her eyes smoldered in anger. "Enough. You were seen with Mage Herrick. A charge has been issued against both of you for having inappropriate relations. It is forbidden for a unicorn keeper and a mage to be involved."

"I saw Mage Herrick with Sabrine. She can vouch we weren't having relations."

Brennah's hand slid across the smooth wood of the table in a circular motion. "Are you saying Sabrine was looking at the tapestries with you?"

She shook her head. "No, I ran into her in the hallway

near the library. Mage Herrick found us there and sent us back to the dorm." At least that part was true.

"This isn't the first night you have snuck out."

"I couldn't sleep."

Brennah's hand stopped moving in a circular motion and her fingers tapped. "You deny having relations with Mage Herrick."

"Yes."

"Were you aware that Herrick is my son?"

She shifted uneasily in her seat. Of course, the person who suspected her magic had to be the son of the Keep Mage. She shook her head. "No, ma'am."

"He is destined to greatness. I will not allow some little peasant to use him to further herself." Brennah rose. Her eyes sparking despite the slits. "Be satisfied with what you have, Trainee Madelen, it is much more than you were born into."

She knew Mage Brennah was trying to insult her, but she was so relieved at not getting caught in what she had truly done that she only nodded.

"I will be watching you. Excused."

She slowly rose and beat a hasty retreat out the door. Mistress Marta waited on the other side. She grabbed Jiline's arm and waited on Brennah.

"She may return to her training. Separate her from the others at night."

Marta nodded and didn't drop her grip as she marched Jiline down. "You might have gotten off easy from the Keep Mage, but don't think I will tolerate your behavior."

Jiline debated arguing the issue and decided she needed to have Marta on her side if she was going to have any chance of helping the unicorns. She didn't know what being separated from the others meant, but had a feeling it would make it impossible for her to sneak down to the valley. "Sabrine lied."

"Did she?" Marta didn't even look at her as they descended the stairs.

"Mage Brennah didn't punish me because she knows I'm innocent of what Sabrine accused me of."

Marta chuckled lightly. "She didn't punish you because she would have to punish her own son. I say we should throw you out into the valley again and have the unicorns judge whether you're innocent or not."

SHE SUPPOSED SHE should be thankful Mage Brennah agreed with Marta's suggestion as she slid down the cliff face to the valley in front of everyone. She was the only trainee going down this time. Mistress Marta had removed her red sash before sending her down. She didn't know where the five keepers currently in the valley were stationed, but she was sure she was being watched and judged. She just hoped the unicorns knew what was going on and wouldn't abandon her. They had to choose her again if she was to have any chance of helping them.

HERRICK MET HIS mother on the patio wondering why she had summoned him away from Lionel's continued quest to convince him to come with him when he left. "Mother?"

She motioned him to stand at the railing and he saw Jiline reach the bottom of the cliff. Yeah, the draw was as strong as ever, but he shoved it in and kept his face from showing what he felt.

"What's going on?"

"Trainee Madelen is being tested again."

He frowned as she walked into the first tree line. The urge to protect was as strong as before, but he didn't act on it. He could control himself. "Why?"

Brennah turned to frown at him. "You aren't the slightest bit worried about her and what the unicorns will do to her."

He shrugged to loosen the tension he felt. "They chose her as a keeper. She's safe down there."

"The keepers aren't ever completely safe in a unicorn's presence."

"Then why send her down before she finishes her training?"

"Charges have been brought up against her."

Herrick kept his gaze on the valley not wanting to give his mother the chance to read his emotions. "Charges of what?"

Her eyes left his profile and went to the valley floor as well. "You didn't tell me you caught her breaking curfew."

"Her and another trainee. I sent them back to their room. You're retesting her because she broke curfew?" He looked at her then. "Isn't that a little extreme?"

Her lips tightened. "I'm not retesting her because she broke curfew."

He almost blurted out, well than why? But held it in, he wasn't supposed to be drawn to her, to care about her anymore than he would care for any other trainee or keeper within the Keep. His mother was toying with him. Would she really risk a possible keeper's safety just to test whether he was still drawn to Madelen? He pushed off from the railing and strolled back to the Keep wall.

"Where do you think you're going?"

He turned back and shrugged. "I didn't realize you wanted me to stay."

"I summoned you here and I have not dismissed you."

"I was in the middle of a potion. I'll have to start over if I leave it for too long."

Her frown was uncertain this time, but her hand beckoned him back to her. With a sigh of pretend nonchalance, he rejoined her and leaned against the railing. Madelen was out of sight. His gut clenched as it had before, but he didn't allow himself to physically react to the sensation.

"She is being retested to make sure she is still pure."

Herrick frowned. "The crystal would be a lot quicker."

She turned and grabbed his arm. "This isn't a joke. You would trifle with this keeper and then send her to be savaged by the unicorns?"

He held up his hands and took a step back. "What? Wait a minute. Are you accusing me of having..." He couldn't quite say it to his mother. "I've left her alone just as you recommended. I haven't touched her."

His mother's eyes were piercing as she stared at him.

"Her life balances on your lies."

He shook his head. "I'm not lying, mother. Why would I jeopardize a unicorn keeper? I know how important they are to the Keep's continued existence. Fewer and fewer keepers are passing the test. Isn't that what you're always telling me?"

Her stare lost its certainty. "You didn't tell me about her breaking curfew."

"I didn't realize it was that important. She isn't the first trainee to violate curfew. If I had realized it would be this big of deal, I would have marched the both of *them* to you right away. Did you send the other girl down there too?"

His mother glanced away. "No, she isn't a unicorn keeper. The unicorns will tell me if you're telling the truth."

JILINE DIDN'T GO where she had discovered the unicorns previously, but headed into the middle of the valley and walked. She might as well drag it out as long as she could. She hadn't been able to spot any of the keepers who would be watching. How could they report on the unicorns mauling her if they didn't witness it first hand? Of course, maybe they would just look for her dead body if she didn't return by nightfall. But the unicorns didn't kill for rejection. They simply refused to show themselves to you.

The unicorn colt stepped into her path. *What is wrong?*

She shook her head and slowed as if she wasn't used to his presence. She ran last night's and today's occurrences through her mind to tell him why she was down in the valley. She also added in her belief that she would be locked up or guarded at night and wouldn't be able to sneak down.

A keeper is to your left behind you watching us from the tallest tree of the forest strip. The unicorn colt walked slowly toward her and she stood still.

She didn't know what to do. How was she supposed to help them if she couldn't even come down to the valley? The unicorn colt wouldn't be able to help her control the magic he had hidden.

Do not worry. We will find a way. Listen for me. I will call to you. The first winter storm is on its way. Come down to the valley after the first snow flakes fall.

She bit her lip. The mages had been clear that once the snow fell no one could leave the Keep or enter the Keep. The trails were impassable.

There will be a window of opportunity. It will slow their pursuit of us. Dress warmly. The unicorn colt suddenly danced around her before flitting back through the meadow and away from her.

Jiline watched the unicorn leave before turning slowly. She could see the keeper now. How she hadn't noticed him before was curious. He climbed down the tree as she walked back into the woods. It was the same keeper who had given her the red scarf in the first place.

He smiled and she realized she didn't know his name. He looked to be about Herrick's age.

"Glad he didn't run you through."

"You were expecting it?" Her sharp retort caught her by surprise.

But that didn't bother him judging by his laugh.

"You're the first keeper who's been sent back in so quickly after selection. I figured there was some reason they were retesting so soon."

Sabrine. She gritted her teeth. The girl had gone from a minor annoyance to a major headache. "Someone likes to spread rumors."

He nodded as if he understood and walked with her back toward the Keep cliff. "Ladies first."

She started to climb and glanced over her shoulder in surprise when she realized he was climbing up behind her. Mistress Marta waited at the top, her frown still in place. The fact that Jiline was still alive didn't appear to have swayed her suspicions.

"Eli?" Mistress Marta questioned.

"They chose her again without hesitation," Eli answered quickly, he saluted and then scrambled back down the cliff face.

Marta's frown deepened and Jiline realized she had fully expected her to be rejected if not hurt by the unicorns. She had believed Sabrine's lies completely. Marta gestured to the hallway. "Your class is currently in the library. I will tell Mage Brennah that you passed the test."

Jiline bobbed her head and ran up the stairs. Upon entering the library and seeing the surprised and angry look on Sabrine's face, she had to suppress the urge to walk over and slap the lying girl. But she wasn't the only one. Everyone appeared to be surprised. They had all believed Sabrine.

10. PROTECTOR

A WEEK LATER the storm the unicorns had foretold arrived. The Keep was ready for it. The last of the visitors were gone a good two days before and the Keep was down to three mages. Mage Brennah, Herrick, and an old woman who arrived just before the last visitor left. Jiline only knew she was a mage based on her robes as she hadn't been introduced to her.

Jiline stood at one of the hallway's windows and watched the rolling clouds approach. The wind was monstrous and she couldn't imagine what it was like for the keepers down in the valley perched in their treetop watch towers.

The other trainees were equally as nervous. This would be the first winter for all of them, and the first time they would be physically if not psychologically locked within the Keep. Mistress Marta had said the snow would get so deep as to completely cover the first story. The doors wouldn't open. If anyone ventured out, which she didn't recommend because you could freeze before anyone found you, they would have to step out of one of the second story windows.

She had been listening for the unicorn's call. She didn't know if he had called and she just couldn't hear or if he still hadn't called. Sabrine stopped in the hallway when she saw her. Jiline turned from the window to glare at her. Sabrine hadn't shown any remorse for her lies and everyone still seemed to believe her even after Jiline had been tested and found innocent. She didn't know how Sabrine had twisted the rumors to keep them going, but judging how the other trainees avoided her she knew they believed her.

The only person who had talked to her without being forced was Eli. He had come looking for her after her second testing to ask what she'd done to earn the wrath of the Keep Mage.

Turning away from Sabrine, she went the rest of the way to the library. The other trainees had gathered and ignored her. It probably didn't help that Sabrine remained in the dormitory room while she was locked up in a single room every night. Yeah, that didn't say much toward her innocence.

She dropped down in the chair by the wall and picked up the book she had been studying earlier. Worry over the beings who devoured the unicorns haunted her dreams. Without the protection of the Keep, would she be releasing the unicorns to a certain death? According to every scroll and book she read, the answer was yes.

But she wasn't being trained to fight them. She didn't know of any way to repel the nasty creatures.

"Madelen," Mistress Marta called from the doorway.

It took her a second to remember to react to the name and she looked up. Eli stood next to Marta and grinned at her.

"Come here," Marta commanded.

The other trainees watched her leave in hushed silence. Marta remained and Eli led her down the hallway.

"Bunch of gossips," Eli whispered under his breath. "Good news."

"It's good that they gossip?"

He laughed. "No, good news that I was able to convince Marta to put you under my care. You're wasted in there."

"What do you mean?" Jiline glanced back at the library doorway.

"Book work doesn't teach you what you need to know to protect the unicorns." Eli led her into a large room without any furniture except for some cabinets on the other side. A large door sat between the cabinets. "But I will."

Her interest piqued. "I thought Marta was our teacher."

"Marta will teach you the ways of the Keep and the unicorn lore, but the keepers choose who they will train. We each have a skill, the five of us."

"But aren't there more than five keepers?"

"But only five keepers in the valley at once. We each serve a purpose." He paused as if waiting for another question.

She obliged him. "And your purpose?"

"I kill the beasties who threaten the unicorns."

Her jaw dropped.

He was enjoying himself as he moved away to open a cabinet filled with deadly weapons. "The mages try to keep it quiet whenever someone or something sneaks past our barriers to kill a unicorn. Most believe the barrier is all that protects them."

Her instincts had been correct. It hadn't made sense to her that all the keepers did was sit and watch the unicorns. Especially since the unicorns hid from them most of the time.

"But when the barrier fails we have to help the unicorns. Some creatures are weak and underestimate the lethal power the unicorns have and they don't need my assistance, but even so. We can't allow a single unicorn to be taken. Other creatures do have the power to take a unicorn down and we intercede before they have the opportunity."

"The pictures on the scrolls?"

He smiled as he pulled out a long metal stick with a sharp point. "I noticed someone had gone through them." He turned to her. "I'd hoped it was you. When I saw how the unicorn danced around you, I knew you were the one I must train."

She bit her lip. "Danced?"

"The unicorns trust us the most. They must if we're to fight alongside them. They know I'll give my life to protect one of them. I can't help protect them if I'm worrying one of them will turn on me. Other keepers stay to the trees.

Though the unicorns tolerate them, they don't trust them as they trust the protectors."

She stared at the weapon cabinet and thought of the task she would be doing shortly. "Show me how."

WEAPON TRAINING WAS almost more difficult than climbing the ropes. Her arms ached and she wasn't sure her hands would function well enough to hold a pen let alone one of the five weapons Eli had schooled her on. She sank to the stone floor. Eli had not excused her yet. He was putting away the swords they had just finished with. She dreaded what he would pull out next to torment her.

She might want to know how to protect the unicorns, but she was beginning to have severe doubts she would ever be capable of such a feat. Her hands rested on the cool stones of the floor. Tempted by them she didn't care how it looked and lay back so she stared at the ceiling. Her breath was still coming too fast.

A high window drew her attention and the clouds had arrived since she had looked outside in the morning. The dark gray was threatening and explained why she was waiting for Eli to call the session for the evening meal. It probably wasn't evening. There were no time pieces in the training room.

Eli suddenly appeared in her vision as he stood over her. He squatted down and she pushed up into a sitting position on her aching arms. A moment ago she hadn't cared, but now she blushed to be caught in such a position.

"Not as easy as you thought?" He smiled.

She shook her head. "I don't know if I can do this."

"Of course you can." Eli shifted and sat cross-legged on the floor. "We've all winter. You'll be ready by spring."

She wished she did have until spring, but that wasn't going to happen.

"We can slow it down now." He propped an arm on his upraised knee. "I needed to check your stamina and drive."

Jiline narrowed her eyes. "Why?"

He cocked his head. He was always in motion. She hadn't seem him still throughout the entire day. "Half of being a protector is going farther than you're physically capable in a moment. You have to fight beyond your exhaustion and fear."

"Exhaustion. Check. Is fear tomorrow?"

He shook his head and rose in a fluid movement. He offered a hand and pulled her up to her feet. "Time for the book work."

She turned and froze when she saw Herrick leaning in the doorway, his permanent frown on his face.

Eli didn't pause, but walked toward him. "Mage Herrick. Can I help you with something?"

"I heard you were training a new recruit." Herrick's voice was soft.

"Trainee Madelen this is Mage Herrick." Eli introduced them like he hadn't heard the rumors which dogged her with everyone else. Had he really not heard the rumors or was he playing some sort of game?

"We've met," Herrick said sharply, his eyes searching

her face before he stepped out of the doorway and from effectively blocking their exit. "I won't keep you."

HERRICK PACED THE magic room in agitation. She was just below him with Eli. He'd always gotten along with the protector before. But seeing him pay so much attention to Madelen was intolerable. He simply couldn't watch without exposing the draw. So he locked himself within the magic room to torment himself where no one could see.

Coming across the two in the training room had caught him by surprise. Seeing Eli leaning over the prone form of Madelen had sent the draw skyrocketing. He kicked a stool against the wall. Girls within the Keep were drawn to Eli and his pretty features. But Eli was devoted to being a unicorn keeper and protector.

Even his mother had commented on how dedicated he was when he'd first been chosen as a protector. They had a high turnover rate when they were that devoted. No sense of self preservation in him. But Eli was as good a fighter as he was devoted.

And he'd picked Madelen out of this class to train. Why?

Herrick turned to look at the scrying mirror. He could peek and see what they were doing in the library. His mother often used a mirror to watch the charges within the Keep. He took a step toward it before stopping. Nothing was going on in the library. It was his own dirty mind tormenting him. Eli's dedication wouldn't allow improper relations between himself and Madelen. It would be the same as standing idly by and watching a dark creature slaughter a unicorn.

"Get ahold of yourself," he whispered between clenched teeth and dropped down in the chair behind the work table. He closed his eyes and concentrated on breathing calmly.

THE MAGE LIGHTS burned brightly within the library. Eli had spread scrolls across the largest table in the center of the great room. Which they had to themselves. She didn't know where the others had gone, but was glad to not have them watching her. She also wondered, if being a protector was so important why was Eli training only her?

"Eli?"

He brought over another scroll and spread it out in front of her. "This is a magdorn. Nasty little guy."

He looked like a contorted frog and she bit her lip to hold her question in.

"What?"

"Why am I the only one training as a protector?"

"I told you. The unicorn chose you as one. I should have realized it the first day when so many of them walked by you without reacting. I assumed it was the other direction." He shrugged. "Protector isn't the only duty of the unicorn keepers. There are also observers. You have to have incredible eyesight to be a watcher. They patrol the perimeter and keep an eye on the wall. Any weakness has to be reported right away. They're often the first to see a creature coming in. There are usually two watchers in the valley at a time."

"How many protectors?"

"One."

"Only one?" She bit her lip. That meant he fought by himself.

He grinned and patted her on the back. "Not as many of us."

"What about the other two keepers within the valley?"

"Caretakers. They make sure the valley's functioning as it should and watch for the first sign of illness within the unicorns."

"They can get sick," She turned to him in surprise. "But they're magical beings. Can't they heal themselves?"

He shrugged. "Occasionally, a unicorn becomes ill. The caretakers try to heal it as best they can." He frowned and ran his hand through his shaggy hair. "But it's always been a lost cause. They make the unicorn as comfortable as possible before death comes."

She stared at him unable to grasp the idea that a unicorn could die. The magic coming off them was so palpable as to be a physical force. If they could heal others with a touch of their horn, why couldn't they heal each other?

Eli began to roll up the scrolls. "It's getting late."

She glanced to the high window and sure enough no more gray clouds just blackness. They had worked through the evening meal. She helped him roll up the remaining scrolls and followed him out of the library.

"Come with me," Eli said and led her down into the

kitchen. A few cloth bundles were set out on the counter. He picked up two and handed one to her. "Meals to go."

She fidgeted with the bundle uncertain of whether she was being excused or would also be eating with him.

"We'll meet directly after breakfast. Can you find the training room on your own?"

She nodded, fairly certain she remembered what hallway he had taken.

"Then I bid you goodnight."

Eli left her as quickly as he tended to do everything. She exited the kitchen at a more leisurely pace walking in the non-flickering mage light until she reached her room. The door was open. Had she missed curfew? No one waited for her as they had the previous nights to lock her in. Perhaps Eli's selection of her to train would prove even more useful than learning to protect the unicorns. Maybe Marta trusted her again.

11. KISS

ELI TRAINED WITH her all day for the next two days. She didn't question why he wasn't down in the valley. She needed to absorb as much as she could in the short amount of time she had. The clouds continued to threaten that time was short, but the promise of snow had not materialized into actual snow. According to Marta, it was unusually warm and all it did was rain and rain.

Each weapon served a purpose. Some creatures could only be killed by a single weapon within the cabinet. For others any weapon would do. She made a cheat sheet. Copying the creatures' pictures from the scrolls to her own and writing down the name of the weapon used. Time compressed around her. There wasn't enough.

Evening was drawing closer and she was being tortured with the swords again. How she hated the swords.

"Can I ask you a question?"

Eli weighed the sword in his hand and gave her an evil grin. "Always ask the questions, Madelen, it's how we learn."

"Why are all the keepers young? The ones who go into the valley that is."

He lowered the sword. "Noticed that, did you?"

She shrugged.

"That's good. Most trainees don't notice until their best friend leaves. Being a keeper takes a lot out of a person, even those who only stay within the Keep. Some keepers aren't as watchful as they should be and a dark creature takes them out. Others have run away in fear. I don't know what happens to them. The mages recruit every couple of years, but try not to go to the same villages so they don't appear to be taking as many as they do."

She considered what he said. "Why do we have to be between ten and fifteen years?"

He glanced away from her before looking back. "It's the pureness test. Less likely to get as many of us if they wait much longer, but any younger than ten and you can't handle the physical aspect of it all."

"How old were you when you were brought here?"

"Eleven."

Her jaw dropped. "You trained to be a protector when you were eleven?"

He shrugged. "As I told you, the unicorns choose who'll be a protector."

"But." She thought of Cris who she hadn't seen very much, trying to avoid her so she wouldn't realize she wasn't Madelen and blow her cover. She couldn't imagine Cris in here, hefting swords and throwing poison darts.

He suddenly moved, swinging his sword. She raised

hers to block his blow and gritted her teeth against the impact as it moved down her back.

THE RAIN HAD turned into a depressing drizzle. She ate her dinner alone again, but didn't return to her room this time. Instead, she sat just within the Keep walls on the mages' patio. She could barely see the valley below, but she watched for any flash of white. The snow hadn't come and she hadn't heard a call from the unicorn colt.

A scuff of a boot warned her she was no longer alone. Somehow she knew who it was before she turned. Herrick stood a few feet away.

Manners dictated she should stand and bow to him, but at the moment she was too tired to care. She nodded her head to acknowledge him before turning back to the night instead. He was always watching her anyway. She'd caught flashes of him the last two days and had wondered when he planned on accusing her of not being Madelen. Something was bothering him about her. But she had no idea how to squash his suspicions. Eli had even noted this afternoon that Herrick seemed to be about a lot.

Herrick cleared his throat and stepped forward so he was in line with her. "Late dinner?"

She nodded, but again held her tongue, uncertain of what to say.

"He's training you too hard."

She glanced up, urged to defend Eli. "Protecting the unicorns is serious business."

His lips curved. "He hasn't been at his post for the last

three days. How is he supposed to protect the unicorns if he isn't down there?"

She frowned at the soft accusation. "He's going down to the valley tomorrow." She didn't add that she would miss him and dreaded being put back into the regular unicorn keeper training class.

He looked back out at the night. "He spent his days off with you."

She glanced at him, but didn't ask the question forming.

It appeared she didn't need to as he volunteered the information. "Keepers aren't slaves, Madelen. You do get a few days off every month to rest or do as you wish. Interesting that Eli would choose to spend his time training you. He'll still have to train you while working a full load. You'll probably have to train with him at night. But you always were a night bird flitting around the dark corridors."

She narrowed her eyes and considered what she should say to him. Because of his constant presence she had to be tested again. Even after the retesting, he was still always around. But this was the first time he had spoken at length with her since discovering her in the hallway with Sabrine.

"Are you trying to get me thrown out as a keeper?"

He looked at the ground. "Why do you think that?"

"You don't like me." She stared out at the black night. "I passed your crystal test twice. I passed the unicorn test twice. Yet, you still watch me as if I don't belong here."

She could see him staring at her out of the corner of her eye, but she kept her gaze firmly on the other side of the valley. Not that she could actually see it.

"I'm not," he paused. "Do you know what a magical draw is?"

She shook her head and tried to remember if it had been talked about in one of the many classes she had sat through so far.

"Don't worry. You aren't supposed to. It's exclusively within the mage traditions and lore."

She stopped watching him from the corner of her eye and turned in confusion. Then why would he have asked her?

"There are those who believe that when two mages who are meant to be together a magical connection forms between the two." He hesitated again. "We call it the draw. When it first appears it can be difficult for the mages to think of anything but each other. In time, they learn to control it, but have difficulty being apart for long."

"You're talking about love," she said, thinking about Wilm and Madelen and what she had done so they could remain together.

"Similar, but not quite. It's a magical connection. It feels physical."

"What if one mage feels it and another doesn't?"

He opened his mouth and then closed it. "I've never heard of such a thing. All the writings describe it as a mutual connection."

She bit her lip trying to understand where he was going with his description.

His eyes were steady on her. "I feel a draw toward

you."

She froze in body and thoughts. "W-what?"

"Impossible you see, because you're non-magical. A draw is only supposed to be felt between two mages." As he spoke, his voice became stronger and more sure. "Yet it won't go away. No matter how much I tell myself you aren't a mage it won't dissipate. And you don't feel it toward me." He shrugged and his lips curved without humor. "You're not a mage and can't feel a draw. So, I suppose you're right and I have to wonder what other mages have done who felt a draw toward someone who didn't reciprocate."

She stared into his eyes and realized he was completely sincere in what he was saying to her. His testing of the crystal suddenly made sense. He was trying to prove to himself that she was a mage like him, but the unicorns had hidden her magic.

Criminy, she had magic within her. Did that mean she could have this draw he spoke of? She didn't have feelings like that toward him. The type of feelings she had seen with Madelen and Wilm. But having magic didn't make her a mage. What had the unicorns said, that most people had some sort of magic within them. That was why the mages had to travel so much to find their keepers. Finding people without magic was more difficult than finding those with magic.

"I've made you speechless." He shook his head and dropped their gaze. "I apologize. I didn't intend to make you uncomfortable, but I could no longer....No, I could have continued to pretend. I didn't want to. Seeing you with Eli was...upsetting. Scrambled my thoughts for a little bit. Made me think it might be possible for a mage and a non-magic to have a draw."

"I..." She stopped uncertain of what to say. She had been so focused on her task at hand, the task that would come before she was ready. She had shoved Herrick out of her mind as much as possible. He had occupied her thoughts too much when she had first arrived at the Keep.

"Don't worry," he breathed deeply, "I won't speak of this with you again. This conversation didn't help as I had thought it would. I'd thought....It doesn't matter."

She found her words then. "Of course it matters." Except for the crystal incident, Herrick hadn't done anything overtly unkind to her and had escorted her up the mountain. It had been others' reaction to his continued presence, not him, which had caused her problems. "What did you think?"

He looked at her again. "That telling you would somehow release me." He rolled onto his feet and crouched next to her. "But alas it hasn't worked. I shall have to think on another solution. Perhaps a spell."

"I'm sorry, Herrick," she whispered, glancing down at her hands.

If she hadn't been staring at her hands, she might have had a chance to react. But as it was he took her completely by surprise when his lips settled on hers. It was a quick kiss. He pulled back almost instantly and walked back into the Keep.

But it might as well have been an eternity for how much it affected her. She couldn't react. Her fingers trembled as they touched her tingling lips.

The snow is coming.

She pressed her lips together and dropped her hand. He had kissed her.

Jiline!

She jumped and realized the unicorn colt was calling her. Biting her lip, she tried to force her thoughts away from Herrick's kiss to the valley floor. Standing up, she walked to the railing.

The snow is coming. We will leave in the first light. You must come before then, but not now. The keepers are nervous.

She nodded. Though she was pretty sure he couldn't actually see her.

Get some sleep now. You'll need it.

She hurried to gather up the remains of her dinner and rushed back to her room.

SLEEPING HAD BEEN difficult, but she had tried as commanded before slipping out in the pre-dawn darkness to the protector training room. She wore her warmest clothes and cloak. The Keep was silent. Fear of being caught made her senses stretch painfully, but she quietly opened the weapon cabinet and selected the weapons she had already decided on.

Two poison darts, a short sword strapped to her waist, and a sharp flying disk. Her own knife was already in her small bag along with two food bundles she had grabbed and her cheat scroll with the hand drawings of the dark creatures. She tip-toed away from the training room to the entryway down to the valley.

The keepers below worried her. She shivered as she stepped out. The snow had arrived. Giant flakes fell on the top of the trail and the mage's patio. Pulling the hood of her cloak up, she began the careful climb down. Amazingly, as she went the temperature rose and no snow fell on the valley floor.

She panicked, wondering if it wasn't as close to dawn as she thought. Had she mis-timed it?

You are right on time.

She looked at the first row of trees. The unicorn colt waited for her. She ran to him feeling awkward with her bag and sword.

Come with me.

She fell into step beside him as he strode out. She had no idea where they were going in the dark, but somehow she didn't trip over any branches or rocks despite not being able to see. The clouds effectively blocked out any moon or star light that might have guided her path. She glanced up at the sky. How could the valley not have any snow? She tested the ground. It had been raining for days. Yet the ground on the valley floor wasn't muddy.

Our valley never gets more than a light drizzle.

She wondered why, but didn't voice her question since the unicorn hadn't told her it was safe to speak. They walked on in silence and she realized that the almost complete darkness was slowly lightening. They reached the place the other unicorns had gathered. They were still as statues and her breath caught in her throat at their beauty and numbers. She started to count them, but the unicorn colt distracted her by touching his horn to her head.

You are now ready.

She panicked. "No, I'm not."

The unicorns all raised their heads.

Don't speak. I can hear your thoughts. Yes, you are. He moved closer and sniffed. *Come with me.*

She followed him up a steep path. Thankfully it was no longer pitch black, but she watched the ground carefully as they climbed. It really wasn't a path, but a spot the unicorn had picked to scale the hill. He stopped suddenly.

The barrier is there. It is weak. We've kept it so, but can not break it.

She had no idea what she was supposed to do.

A mage touched you tonight.

She remembered what Mage Brennah had said about being of pure body. Had she ruined everything from not stopping Herrick from kissing her? She nodded.

His magic clings to you. It is not tainted with unicorn magic.

She blinked in surprise at the idea that unicorn magic could be called tainted by a unicorn.

You can use it along with your own.

She shook her head, still not understanding.

We don't have a lot of time. The keepers are becoming anxious at not spotting any of us. The unicorn colt turned his head. *Well, most of the keepers. Clear your thoughts.*

She closed her eyes and did her best.

Hold your hands up toward the weak part of the wall. Can you feel it?

She faced the barrier and held her hands up, and tried to feel whatever it was she was supposed to feel. Her fingers tingled. She pulled back, surprised.

Good, hands up, feel the vibrations of the barrier. They are not resonating in harmony. You feel the discord.

She bit her lip and slowly raised her hands again bracing herself for the sharp tingle. It took a moment, but she thought she felt a slight ripple in the pattern.

You must thrust your magic into the discord and hold it. Build a hole. We will slip through the hole.

She nodded and tried to thrust her magic, but nothing happened.

The colt snorted. *Can you feel the mage's magic on you?*

She hesitated and wrinkled her nose, before shaking her head.

The colt bumped her in agitation. *Try harder.*

Taking a deep breath, she thought of Herrick's kiss, her lips tingled. The tingle spread across her body.

Good. Now your magic. It should feel different.

A warmth became present in her body.

Merge them together.

Another deep breath and she soothed the tingling into the warmth.

Thrust.

She followed the unicorn colt's words and this time actually felt a slice go through the barrier.

Hold it.

The unicorn colt turned his head and cloven hooves raced up the short trail. White flashed past her as they leapt through the hole she had created. The unicorn colt bumped her with his nose as she stared dumbfounded.

Us next.

He pushed her through the hole. Walking through her own magic was a weird experience and she almost stopped, but his steady pressure on her back forced her through the icky feeling.

You'll need to close it now.

She turned back to look at the hole. Eli stood at the foot of the trail on the other side of the hole. His expression was surprised.

"Colt!"

He will not trouble you. Close the hole.

Eli didn't move from his position as she tried to yank her magic out as she had thrust it in. It didn't budge.

Ease it out. You want it to return to you.

She didn't want to close her eyes and not know what Eli was doing, but she did and her magic flowed back into her.

Come!

She opened her eyes and turned away from the trail and Eli. A steeper trail greeted her, which the unicorn colt climbed slowly. The other unicorns were long out of sight. The snow fell heavily. She scrambled after him, pulling her cloak tight.

The forest quickly wrapped around them and she worried over what she had done. Where were the other unicorns?

Do not worry. They are just ahead of us. We must move swiftly to beat the snow.

The snow poured down on them.

Yes, but it has not blocked the trails yet.

12. ESCAPE

T HE ALARM WENT up in the Keep, Herrick jumped out
of bed and raced on autopilot to pull his robes on and
shove his feet into boots. The bells had never wrung in the
Keep as long as he had lived there. His first thought went
to Madelen. The draw was tight. His chest constricted. She
wasn't within the Keep.

He raced out of his room and down to the main level
where all the trainees and most of the keepers were
gathering.

His mother stood with Mage Taika and Mistress Marta.
He wasn't surprised the trainees didn't seem to notice him.
The bells were blooming loud. He used their blaring to
control the draw. Shove it down as he did every day.
Madelen missing wasn't enough for his mother to set the
bells. Something else must have happened.

Her gaze was sharp as he joined them.

"What's happened?" he asked.

"The unicorns are gone," his mother whispered. Her
sharp gaze moved from him to the crowd gathered.

He blinked. "They hide sometimes."

"The barrier has been breeched by the unicorns."

"That's impossible."

"Yes, it is." Brennah shook her head. "Marta, we need a full head count of everyone. We need to know who assisted the unicorns."

Where was Madelen? "Something could have broken them out."

His mother didn't answer them as Marta stepped away and began to gather the trainees and the house keepers. There wasn't a single unicorn keeper present.

Mage Taika covered her ears with her hands. "Could someone turn off that infernal racket?"

Brennah raised her own hand and the bells stopped. Herrick blinked at the sudden silence and his magic welled within him. He smashed it down. A few unicorn keepers suddenly appeared, sweaty and muddy.

Eli stepped up to Brennah and bowed his head. "We've swept the valley. Not a single unicorn remains."

"Did you find the breach?"

He shook his head, his eyes trained on the floor.

She stepped menacingly forward. "You are a protector. How could you have allowed this to happen?"

His head lowered farther. "I didn't see. I take full responsibility."

His mother's eyes were narrowed and little sparks shot from her fingers. "I should kill you for your incompetence, but then where would the unicorns be? I'll need every unicorn keeper to search for them. Gather horses. Their trail will be covered quickly by the snow."

Eli bobbed his head before turning on his heel and striding away. Herrick narrowed his eyes. He could have sworn the keeper's lips were curved into a small smile.

Mistress Marta appeared just as Eli vanished down the hallway with several keepers by his side.

"Trainee Madelen is missing."

Brennah frowned and shook her head in irritation. "I knew there was something about that girl." Her glare turned to her son. "Where is she?"

He feigned innocence and shook his head. "How would I know?"

"Search the Keep," Brennah boomed out. "All trainees go to the dining room at once. Keepers, search the Keep, find Trainee Madelen."

Herrick needed to get away from his mother. Her magic bombarded him with her temper. She was quickly losing control and her lack of control was wreaking havoc with his own. He stepped away, relieved when she didn't immediately demand his attention. He ran back up to the magic room and shut himself in.

What had Madelen done? Was her disappearance connected to the unicorns? It was too much of a coincidence to assume otherwise.

He shouldn't have left her out on the patio. Why hadn't he suspected what she was about to do? Of course, what the heck had she done? She had no magic. He stopped in the middle of the floor and closed his eyes. Of course, she had magic.

They were so stupid. He should have trusted the draw more than a crystal. He glared at a bowl of them, so relied on by the mages to know who in their presence might challenge them. Madelen had found a way to trick the crystal. If the mage's had found a way to reverse the crystal's glowing long ago to glow when someone didn't have magic, she must have had a spell to swap it back to its original purpose of glowing when in the presence of magic.

He went to the bookshelf and pulled out the old volume he had studied to understand the draw and why he felt it toward her. He scanned the text in a new way knowing she did have magic. He should be able to use the draw to find her.

He would have to find her before his mother did.

JILINE STUMBLED, BUT righted herself quickly. The unicorn colt remained by her side, supporting her as they moved through the ever deepening snow. Her feet were frozen, but she tried to ignore the numb feeling. The unicorns had stopped ahead and she gave a sigh of relief as the colt stopped next to the group.

Her sigh turned to a squeak of surprise when she saw why they had stopped. Her pony stood under a tree, protected from the snow, saddled and ready to go. She glanced around the clearing. No one but the unicorns.

"Ginger." She ran the few steps to reach her and wrap her arms around her. "How?"

She turned to the colt who stood next to her. Ginger was sweaty and shivering. He touched his horn to her and

Ginger seemed to magically recover from the long run she had obviously endured.

Eli set her free before coming into the valley.

"Eli?" He'd watched her set the unicorns free.

We knew you would need a horse to ride. Eli has been the most connected with us of all protectors. My mother...

The colt's mother walked forward. *I only suggested, not compelled. Eli has always belonged to us more than the mages. He would have set us free himself if he had been able. But he could assist you. We must go now. Reach the snow line before it is too late.*

Jiline gave Ginger another hug and mounted her beneath the tree. Her hands hurt from the cold and she fumbled with the reins. The colt touched his horn to her arm flooding her entire body with warmth.

Enough, the colt's mom said. *If they need assistance ask another, you must not deplete your magic.*

The unicorn colt bobbed his head, but waited for Ginger to break free from the tree at a smart trot before moving off to follow the herd. He stayed next to them which Jiline was thankful for. She could just barely make out the mass of unicorns in front of her through the falling snow. Ginger wasn't used to it either. She snorted and tossed her head occasionally to shake off the layer of snow which gathered on them as they went.

THE KEEPERS HAD gone on the hunt. Herrick watched them leave in the heavy falling snow. He held his hand out to catch a giant flake to analyze it. The hint of magic evaporated. The unicorns had brought in a snow storm to cover their escape.

He dropped his hand as his mother stepped out to stand next to him. She had gotten her magic under control, but he could feel it rippling inside her.

"Mistress Marta will remain here with the trainees and house keepers."

He raised an eyebrow waiting for her to continue.

Her eyes were steady on him. "Madelen?"

Prepared for her question, he didn't outwardly react to Madelen's name. "You haven't found her?"

"You know we haven't."

He shrugged despite her being correct. "How would I know that?"

"The draw would tell you."

"We both agreed what I felt for Madelen was an infatuation not a mage draw," he reminded her, aiming his expression and tone for nonchalance.

"I've changed my mind."

Of course she had. He forced a laugh. "I haven't. It was an infatuation."

"Do not lie to me." Her magic surged within her and he stepped back in alarm.

"I'm not." He forced his own magic not to respond to the possible threat.

Her eyes narrowed. "You're upset."

"So are you, blaming me for a trainee's absence isn't going to help matters." He stepped away from her and sliced his hand to block her magic prickling against him. "I don't know what you expect me to do."

"You could track her with the draw."

He sighed. "I don't feel a draw toward her." The out and out lie came easier and easier. He had never concealed anything from his mother before. Not only was she his mother, but the Keep Mage. Both demanded honesty from their subordinates. Yet, he lied without a single hesitation. "You know, you could lose every single keeper in that snow storm."

His mother looked at the rising snow in alarm. She did as he had. Held her hand out to catch a flake. Except, she cursed and dropped it like it burned. "What would you have me do? Let them escape?"

He considered her word choice. "Why would they want to escape if we're their protectors?"

She glared at him. "Unicorns are very much like children. You know we protect them from the dark creatures and humans who would kill them for their magic."

"Yes, I know, but you keep saying they escaped, not that they were stolen." He caught another snow flake. "This is unicorn magic. I've been around enough mages bolstered by unicorn magic to recognize the feel. But this is pure magic not unicorn mage magic."

She took a deep breath. "Whether they were stolen or escaped isn't the point. The point is they're vulnerable outside of the valley. They will be hunted down and killed. We have no way of protecting them and preserving their magic."

JILINE LOOKED DOWN at the path Ginger followed and the rising snow beside them. The snow didn't seem to be falling as hard as it had before. She slipped the hood off her head and looked at the sky. Snowflakes filled the air above her, but they drifted to the side as if sliding down a steep roof point to the ground.

There were only a couple of inches of snow on the trail, while a few feet away it was already over a foot. She glanced behind her at the unicorn colt. He was bringing up the rear and she was pretty sure he was annoyed at being slowed by the pony.

"We aren't being snowed on," she said.

His head didn't change position. *No. We are far enough from the valley to make the trail easier without risk of discovery.*

She looked back up at the gray sky. Amazed to see the snowflakes fall and then turn away from them. After awhile, her neck began to ache and she stopped looking up, but focused on what was in front of them. Ginger had to trot here and there to keep up with the unicorns' ground-covering walk. But she'd always had to trot when taken out with horses. This time Jiline didn't have to urge her forward so they didn't get left behind.

What did Ginger think of the unicorns? She hadn't shied away when the unicorn colt had touched her with his horn. She treated them the same as she would have treated other horses. Except. She realized Ginger hadn't been doing any neighing or nickering like she normally did. She was unusually silent. Ginger always enjoyed talking with any horses she passed by. Her family joked that Ginger had to get the first and last word in.

Could the unicorns speak to her as well? She turned back to the colt.

Yes. He answered her before she could ask the question. *She understands the necessity to be quiet.*

Was he rebuking her for speaking earlier?

No. You may vocalize your questions if that is easier for you. We are far enough away that if we keep moving they won't be able to catch us.

"How did she make it to that tree to meet us?" She smoothed a hand over Ginger's rump in her contorted position.

She was easy to speak with. There aren't as many mage protections on the stable as there are on the Keep.

She turned forward again and considered how they had gotten Eli to saddle her up. The unicorn mare had forbidden the colt from compelling her into helping them. She was pretty sure she had helped them of her own free will, but if they could compel someone why hadn't they done it before she came to the Keep.

We needed your magic. We couldn't have asked just anyone. The mages are very careful about not leaving the safety of the Keep so we cannot manipulate them into assisting us.

"But I thought," she turned back to face them, "that you didn't tolerate magic in another being and the mages couldn't go down for fear of being killed."

We haven't killed you.

She didn't consider herself to have magic and had already forgotten that small fact.

A story the mages made up to protect themselves. We might kill them for coming near us, but it has nothing to do with the magic within them and everything to do with our imprisonment.

Jiline bit her lip, doubting that she really had magic like the mages despite what she had done in the unicorns' valley. The unicorn colt seemed to believe she had true magic within her. She glanced back at him about to ask how she could have magic now when she hadn't before. The question on the tip of her tongue, she stumbled slightly in thought. She kept wanting to call him by a name, but didn't know if it would insult him to ask. What if they didn't use names?

He tossed his head and snorted. *You may call me Bai.*

It seemed such a simple name for such a magnificent creature of pure magic. The silence of the forest was broken by a river's roar. She glanced forward again and picked up Ginger's reins, uncertainty flowing through her. The trees broke open to reveal a raging river. This was not the same one she had crossed to reach the Keep. At least, she didn't think it was. She had no idea where they were. It hadn't seemed to matter before, but she didn't know how long she would be with the unicorns.

We will be traveling together until you are safely away from the mages reach for assisting us. Do not worry.

She almost laughed at the reassurance. The worry came and went. She trusted the unicorns, but not the sudden adventure she found herself in. Ginger picked her way over the rocks just as the unicorns did to drink from the rushing water. Dismounting, she looked up and then down the river. The snow fell steadily about twenty feet from them almost like they were in an invisible box. She couldn't see outside the box, but within it though cold it was clear and the snow seemed to melt ever so slightly in the box.

Did it push the snow away as they went? The snow was only a few inches deep here as well. But outside the box it continued to climb to feet.

Two unicorns separated from the herd and approached them. Jiline froze. Uncertain if her mental questions had made them angry. Ginger reacting to her uncertainty, raised her head, but a whinny didn't emerge.

Are you cold? It was the unicorn mare's voice.

She considered. "I'm all right."

The unicorn mare briefly touched noses with Bai. *My son tells me you wish to know our names.*

"I—" She started to protest, feeling as if she had overstepped some sort of human-unicorn boundary.

We know your name, Jiline. You may know ours. I am Gwyn. The unicorn mare didn't move away, but stood by Bai and she assumed they were talking directly with each other.

She crouched down, knowing she needed to drink, but loath to put her fingers in the frigid water. It wasn't as cold as she had expected and she drank.

The unicorns started moving off again, picking their way along the river. She checked her girth and remounted Ginger to follow behind them. Gwyn briefly touched her horn to Ginger before rejoining the herd. Ginger filled with energy as she had before and eagerly trotted off to keep up with the unicorns. Bai stayed behind her.

The unicorns and their magical box cleared a path for Ginger making it fairly easy going for them. She looked up at the sky again, a mass of swirling white about ten feet above her head. How did it work?

Herrick would probably know. Her lips tingled at the thought of him. And she pushed them together to get the feeling to stop. He was a mage. He had kept the unicorns against their will. She stumbled over the thought. Why had they kept the unicorns confined?

To bolster their power. The barrier fed off our magic. Not only to sustain itself, but the mage's could pull our magic from the barrier to increase their own power. Your Herrick had not begun to do this. His magic was pure human.

She remembered him saying Herrick's magic wasn't tainted by unicorn magic.

Neither is yours.

But how could unicorn magic be tainted?

When our magic is taken by another creature it is no longer ours – it becomes tainted in our eyes.

She shivered as a wind blew through the magical box. Snow plummeted to the ground blown off the tree branches around the magical box. She glanced up at the sky, uncertain of the time, or even how long they had been riding. They were still going downhill for the most part with flat areas here and there. The river cut out a path in the canyon which the unicorns followed.

13. WYVERNS

H ERRICK WONDERED HOW much longer his mother
would be able to contain herself. The rage had been
steadily growing. The keepers had yet to return or send a
message back and night would fall within the hour. Mistress
Marta stopped in the doorway of the hall and shook her
head.

"She must have taken everything when she left," Marta
said.

Brennah frowned. "What about her bed blankets?"

"They're gone as well."

Brennah growled and tossed a jar across the room. She
had been preparing a tracking potion to find Madelen, but
she needed something of hers, even a hair would do.

"How did she know?" Brennah growled.

Madelen hadn't. Herrick had removed what was left
himself to make sure his mother couldn't track her. He was
just lucky the thought had occurred to him before it came
to his mother.

He walked over to the window to look down into the

valley. Snow blanketed the valley floor. Amazing how nature immediately knew the unicorns were no longer present. The snow would fill the valley in the first time in almost two hundred years.

Keeper Brody hesitated just behind Marta.

Brennah saw him out of the corner of her eye and turned to him. "Well?"

"Her pony and tack are gone," Brody said stiffly. "But I don't know she's the one who took it. The unicorn keepers took all the horses. Perhaps they took the pony as well."

Herrick considered. It was plausible, but he knew his mother didn't believe it. "If she took her pony..."

His mother turned to him.

He continued. "She couldn't have gotten her pony to the valley floor. How would she have helped the unicorns and taken her pony? Our entire side of the valley is one giant cliff. If she has her pony she ran away. Maybe she took advantage of our distraction of the unicorns going missing. You gathered all the keepers in the hall. It would have been easy for her to get to the stable without anyone seeing her and leaving."

Brennah shook her head not agreeing with him. "I don't believe in coincidence. She's the only one missing. She was involved."

Herrick hesitated. "You want her to be involved. It would be simpler." She glared at him. "But the truth is you don't know how the unicorns escaped. Maybe the barrier finally failed. Maybe another mage got tired of having to ask you to use unicorn magic and broke the barrier. Maybe a dark creature broke through and the unicorns took advantage of the hole. We don't know what happened."

"Leave us," Brennah commanded, her gaze steady on her son. Brody and Marta stepped out of the room and the door shut. "You're very determined to prove Madelen's innocence."

He sighed and looked back out the window. He had to be careful with how much he protested and showed on Madelen's behalf. If she realized he felt a draw for her, she would use him to track down Madelen. "Or, your theory is that a unicorn keeper who doesn't have a drop of magic somehow stole her pony, brought the barrier down, and helped the unicorns escape all in the course of the few minutes the unicorn keepers didn't see."

Brennah's gaze didn't waver and practically burned a hole in his back. "She could have fooled us."

"She couldn't have fooled the unicorns. They chose her as a keeper, twice. You know as well as I do that they don't tolerate other magical creatures. They avoid them mostly, but when confronted will attack to preserve their own magic."

Brennah stopped glaring at her son and sat in one of the high backed wooden chairs at the table. Magical books were spread out across the surface. Her voice no longer held the power or rage it had a moment ago. "You have no idea, son, what will happen if we cannot bring the unicorns back to the valley?"

He turned around and walked cautiously to the table.

"Tell me."

Brennah slowly paged through one of the large leather books. "We have been in charge of the unicorns, protecting them in exchange for the use of their magic to bolster ours, for hundreds of years. The Keep is nothing but an isolated stone fortress without the presence of the unicorns." Her fingers tightened into a fist. "They escaped under my watch. The other mages will remove me as soon as the news reaches them. Our power base will be shattered. We'll go back to the days where we had to bow and grovel doing tricks to earn a place in some fat king's castle."

"Just because the unicorns are gone doesn't mean we are nothing," he whispered. He could still feel his own magic within. He didn't depend on the unicorns to make him stronger.

She glanced up and frowned. "You're so young, Herrick. You have not felt what it is like to be bolstered by unicorn magic. I can feel it draining from me as we speak. The barrier continues to crumble without them to keep it strong."

"It's still there?" He'd assumed since the snow was in the valley floor that the barrier was gone.

"It slowly retreats, taking with it the last of the unicorn's magic." Brennah sat still for a moment. "We have lost all of our unicorn keepers as well. None have returned in the storm. They will freeze to death before they can make it around the mountain to the other side of the valley where the unicorns broke free."

"You know where they escaped?"

Brennah stood. "There was a hole in the barrier on the north side of the valley. It has to be where they left."

He frowned. "Did you send any keepers after them through the hole?"

She closed her eyes. "No, you heard me send them all on horseback. You see why the other mages will remove me. I panicked. I didn't think thoroughly through the crisis. Now I can see what I should have done, but it is too late."

Brennah walked over to look down at the valley through the window.

"We could still go through the hole." Herrick felt compelled to point out.

"On foot?" Brennah shook her head. "The unicorns have been gone since daybreak. We could never catch them on foot. If I had sent a few keepers immediately, perhaps, but now, they wouldn't even be able to track them."

The soft gray of daylight was fading into a muted gray. Brennah turned away from the window and strode to the table. "I will not give up."

No, she wouldn't. Herrick left her to her spell casting and went to his room. Gathering his belongings, he prepared to ride. His mother was wrong. They could track the unicorns. He wasn't sure how long it would take her to realize her mistake, but he had to get to Madelen before she did.

Night had fallen before something drew him from his room. Herrick stopped at the top of the stairs watching the wet and freezing unicorn keepers stand dejectedly in front of his mother. It looked like they had been turned back by the storm. His mother should have been glad that she hadn't lost all of her unicorn keepers, but instead she raged at them, pelting them with magical punishment, judging by how the keepers in front flinched again and again.

He jogged down the stairs to distract her wrath. It wasn't their fault and it was unfair of her to take her rage out on them. He stepped into her path. The magical lash stung, but he didn't flinch.

Her hands stopped waving and seeing his glare, she dropped them by her side. She turned and returned to the great room where she had sequestered herself with her books.

Mistress Marta stood hidden inside one of the hallways. He gestured her out. "They need food and warm clothes."

Her eyes widened at his orders, but her head bobbed. "Come with me."

One of the unicorn keepers, didn't go. It was Eli.

Herrick raised an eyebrow. Eli was just as frozen as the others and as one of those in front had taken the bulk of Brennah's rage. "What is it, Eli?"

"The trail was impassable."

He nodded. "You told my mother."

Eli slowly shook his head. "She wouldn't allow me to speak. We went as far as the horses could swim. But the snow was up to their bellies. I made the decision to turn back. The others were listening to my orders."

Eli wished the blame to be put on himself. Herrick considered and thought about the many hours Eli had spent with Madelen. If she had assistance in escaping, most likely it would have come from Eli. The unicorns trusted the protectors the most. He wondered why his mother hadn't considered the possibility of one of the protectors in assisting them in their escape.

"You made the right decision," Herrick said, keeping his thoughts to himself. "Eat and warm up."

Eli bowed his head at the dismissal and walked slowly away. Herrick waited until he was out of sight before going back up the stairs where he had dropped his bundle of winter clothes, food, and magical gear. Going down to the Keep patio, he stored them against the wall before leaning out over the railing to look down to the valley floor. To get a horse down there would be incredibly difficult. He narrowed his eyes as he considered how much energy it would take out of him. Too much. But he couldn't go on foot either.

The trails would be impassable. The snow shoes were too bulky to do anything more than move about the Keep grounds. He had to make time. He looked up at the clouds. The snow fell heavily and would probably for some time. Catching a flake, he felt the unicorn's magic as it melted. If the storm was magic-encouraged perhaps he could encourage it to die down with a little more magic. He was tempted to dismiss the idea at first since his mother hadn't tried.

But his mother wasn't exactly at peak form right now. In fact, he would guess she wasn't thinking critically about the problem at all. Sending all the unicorn keepers into a snow storm a day's journey from where the unicorns had escaped showed she wasn't thinking clearly.

JILINE PRESSED HERSELF against Ginger's body and shivered. They had camped in the snow for the night. With the unicorns surrounding her the cold had been tolerable, but now they were up and moving around. The wind was howling. The snow blew up from the ground and pelted her face. She didn't understand why the magical box was no longer over them, but would never dare ask.

Bai touched his horn to her shoulder and warmth flooded through her.

"Thank you," she whispered and finished tightening Ginger's girth as she had been doing before the cold had overwhelmed her.

He seemed to give a horse shrug before tapping Ginger as well.

Gwyn walked up to them. She could now distinguish her from the herd by sight not just voice.

The unicorn herd began to move down the river.

I will stay with Jiline for a while. You go on up with the herd.

Bai shook his head, but did as the mare ordered.

"Did I do something wrong?" Jiline asked as Ginger picked her way through the boulders to keep up with the herd.

No, why do you think so?

It was harder to talk with Gwyn than it had been to speak with Bai. She had grown used to his presence and to say what she was thinking.

It is my son, not you. He is too tempted to use his magic to keep you and Ginger moving and warm. He needs to rest a little and replenish. I will keep you moving. Gwyn paused. *It is important that you call on us if need be. I have told the others to tell you their names if you call on them. Do not be afraid to do so. We owe you a great debt.*

Jiline shook her head in denial.

Gwyn's voice held a smile. *Yes, we do. Do not think so little of yourself, young girl child. You did something great, which many would not do, and at personal peril to yourself. I would not have judged you if you had chosen to remain at the Keep for the rest of your life.*

And theirs. The unicorn mare didn't say it, but Jiline thought it. The unicorn herd suddenly stopped, all heads raised. Gwyn snorted and Bai galloped back to them.

"What's wrong?" she asked, looking around at the swirling snow. She hadn't noticed that the magical barrier had been brought back up as they traveled, but the box effect was clear now.

Bai edged closer to Ginger. *I will protect you.*

"Against what?" She reached down to her pack which she had tied to her saddle like a saddle bag.

You smell it? Gwyn asked.

Bai curled his lip. *They are close.*

Her fingers touched the case with the poison darts and she opened it to draw one out. Gwyn snorted next to her, but didn't move.

It is a pack of wyverns. They must have smelled the magic.

Jiline's fingers trembled and she shoved the dart back

into the case and instead unsheathed the small sword she had almost forgotten. Ginger shifted beneath her. Gathering her reins tightly with one hand, she looked where the unicorns focused. They were trapped in the canyon the river carved.

Eli had mentioned the wyverns specifically when they had looked at the scrolls. They lived within the forest and constantly tested the barrier for weakness. Feasting on unicorn flesh would give the wolf-like creatures great power. Their steady diet of non-magical creatures didn't satisfy the hunger they always felt.

The unicorns galloped forward out of the river's path and into the woods. Bai bumped Ginger forward and Jiline released the reins a fraction to allow the pony to race through the deep snow. Gwyn surged in front of her to part the drift and give Ginger a trail. For their strain, the snow slowed them considerably. The barrier dropped as Ginger was engulfed within the unicorn herd. Bai stayed behind her.

As one, the group continued its brisk pace, Jiline and Ginger in the center, Bai beside her. She couldn't spot Gwyn any longer. Shadows moved among the trees they passed.

She raised her sword up, but the unicorns didn't slow. "Bai?"

We see them. They are pacing us. Waiting for a sign of weakness and opportunity to take one of us down.

The wyverns made no noise, at least none that Jiline could hear over the sound of the breathing unicorns. The snow muffled their hoof falls and the unicorns were silent as they prepared for battle.

The shadows moved. Suddenly emerging from the trees, black shapes with sharp teeth and glowing brown eyes streaked toward the herd. She tried to count them as Ginger reared beneath her. Clamping her legs, she rode the rear. The unicorns no longer ran, but turned to face the wyverns.

Snorts and trumpeting neighs filled the air as the unicorns met their enemy. She didn't know what to do. Ginger danced beneath her in fear, but the pony turned where she directed. But what could she do? The wyverns were massive. Much larger than a wolf. And they obviously knew their prey as they darted out of the way of the unicorns horns and hooves.

A streak of black headed toward her and she remembered what Eli had said. They preferred to eat magical meat. She had magic within her. Ginger's feet stilled and Jiline lowered her sword to point it directly at the wyvern.

Bai leapt between them, his horn thrusting up into the wyvern's rib cage. It howled as Bai slid on his haunches and threw the wyvern against a tree. The crunch was awful. She flinched, but didn't have a moment to do more than that before Bai was urging Ginger forward again. The unicorn herd was off. Several wyverns lay bleeding in the snow, and she didn't know where the others had retreated.

She gripped her sword waiting for the next attack as they moved through the woods. But an attack didn't come.

"Bai?"

They retreated when they realized we were not easy targets. They prefer to catch a unicorn alone.

She nodded, but didn't resheath her sword. Ginger huffed and puffed beneath her to keep up with the gallop the unicorns had fallen into. Gwyn dropped back and her horn, also bloody, brushed Ginger's neck.

You are safe now, Jiline. Gwyn's eyes looked directly at her.

She reluctantly and with some difficulty resheathed her sword. The unicorns had handled the wyverns without a problem. She quickly counted the moving herd. They all remained.

"Were any of you hurt?"

No. Gwyn said. *Wyverns do not have magic of their own. They attack physically. Easy to defend against with our numbers. I'm surprised they attacked, but I suppose they were hungry.*

Bai snorted. *They were after her.*

Gwyn dropped back to her son. *Are you sure?*

One of them slipped through the line to take her down. I almost didn't see him in time.

Gwyn was quiet as she moved back up next to Jiline. *I apologize. We should have realized they would try to take you down.*

Her hands trembled and she fisted them before leaning over a little to rub them into Ginger's mane. She held the reins loosely, her body moving automatically with her pony. "Eli said they prefer magical meat. I didn't think I had much in me."

Bai snorted. *Not fun to think of yourself as meat. I told you she had power within her.*

Gwyn's eye rolled. *So you did. But it hasn't fully manifested.* "What do you mean?"

Humans are different from other magical creatures. Most are born with magic as I told you, but very few ever learn to utilize the magic within them. If they can, it begins to emerge as they grow older. The older the mage the more powerful he or she can be.

"But I'm already fifteen years," she protested.

A child. Gwyn snorted and slowed as the herd ahead of them did to a trot. *Your Herrick...*

That was the second time Gwyn had referred to Herrick as hers. The urge to protest was strong.

Is very strong for his age. He would have been stronger than his mother if she had allowed him to use the unicorn magic as she did. But she prevented it to keep him within her control. Most mages do not come to their full powers until about twenty years. That is when they arrive at the Keep to learn to mix their own magic with ours. Herrick was strong enough several years ago. A good five years before the other mages.

How old was Herrick? She knew he was older than she, but had originally assumed he was fifteen until she had learned he was a mage.

Seventeen of your years. Bai said.

"How old will I be for this magic to manifest?"

Bai didn't respond right way. *I believe we sped the process up by helping you open the barrier.*

"You said the barrier couldn't be opened with unicorn magic."

It wasn't. It was opened by your magic, but I gave you a little push in being able to wrap the residual of Herrick's magic with your own.

Bai! Gwyn scolded. *You did not tell us.*

She is untrained and was having difficulty. It was the quickest way to open the barrier.

Gwyn's disapproval radiated out of her.

"What's wrong?"

Nothing, child. Mixing magic is generally not a good idea. There can be after effects.

"What do you mean? What kind of after effects?"

How did Herrick's magic cling to you? Had he cast a spell near you or...on you?

Jiline shook her head. But she realized she had no clue if he had been casting a spell the last time she had seen him. "I assumed," she bit her lip, "when Bai said his magic was on me that it was because Herrick...kissed me."

Gwyn didn't appear to react to the news. But had probably already listened to her thoughts before she had said the words. *Interesting. Mages usually don't share magic through simple touch. Perhaps he had cast a spell before coming upon you.*

Jiline shrugged.

Bai suddenly danced beside them. *Look.*

She did as he bade and squinted her eyes to see what he was gesturing to. But she wasn't sure.

The snow line.

That was when she realized the snow was lighter on the trees and it did look like there wasn't any snow on the ground farther down the trail. She looked around, past the magical box. Sure enough the snow was only a few inches deep and the flurries weren't really snow flakes, but a mix of rain and snow. The unicorns picked up their pace again and finally galloped out of the last of the snow into the muddy dirt and rain. The magical box didn't do much for the mud as they sloshed down the trail, but even Jiline's mood rose knowing they were coming out of the mountains. The grass hills would appear soon.

The magical box prevented her from becoming soaked in the pouring rain just as it had prevented her from freezing in the snow. The trees were beginning to thin and she started to wonder. Where would the unicorns go? Where could they hide?

"Bai, where are we going?"

Bai chewed on some leaves he had just snatched from a tree as they passed. *Home.*

"The valley wasn't your home?" Of course not, it had been their prison.

It was long ago before the mages found us. There are other enchanted forests. We are not the only unicorns within the world.

She hadn't even thought on whether there were other unicorns and where they would be. "So you are going to them?"

Bai hesitated. *No. We do not know where they are.*

"Then where are we going?"

He raised his head and pricked his ears. *Home.*

She bit her lip, not understanding, but she didn't question him again.

You are confusing her. Gwyn said as she dropped back

from the herd. *She doesn't feel it as we do. You see, Jiline, we have felt our new home for some time. It has called out to us in our dreams for years. Welcomed us as soon as we made the decision to escape. We go to those woods where we will live in peace.*

Jiline nodded, but still didn't totally understand. But she believed the unicorns knew where they were going and that was what was important.

14. WEATHER SPELL

H ERRICK DIDN'T LIKE the conclusion he had come up with. He'd found the weather spell, but he wasn't powerful enough to cast it on his own. He would need the help of his mother and Mage Taika to cast it successfully. He had hoped to be able to cast it in the night and sneak off before anyone realized he'd created a heat wave. Didn't look like his plan would work that way. Which meant his mother would send the keepers out again with him.

He couldn't find Madelen with the keepers so close to him. But it was the only way he would be able to leave the Keep. But if he could leave the Keep so could the keepers and his mother. He sat in the magic room pacing back and forth throughout the day. His mother didn't come looking for him so he was left alone to torture himself with deciding what was right.

The draw had become painful. He rubbed his chest as his lungs constricted. A panic attack had seized him about halfway through the day and he'd passed out from lack of oxygen. When he had awakened the pressure on his lungs had eased a bit. But they were increasing again.

He closed his eyes and imagined the air flowing through his lungs unobstructed. He could not have another panic attack. He had to stay in control if he was going to be able to help Madelen. But what would help her more? He was beginning to think pushing the unicorns' storm to even heavier was the best plan. No one but the Keep knew the unicorns and Madelen had escaped. She would be safer if news didn't spread, but the more his thoughts went in that direction the tighter his lungs became.

Shoot, could he physically stand to have her apart from him and in danger? His lungs seized. He pulled at his shirt even though he knew that wasn't going to help as he struggled for air. Snapping his eyes open, he stumbled to the table and grabbed the elixir he had made up earlier and tried to drink it. His hands shook, spilling the liquid, but some made it into his mouth.

His vision blurred. His knees buckled. He dropped the bottle to grab on to the table, but he had no strength and banged against it. A small breath went through. He concentrated on that. Just breathe stupid.

Slowly, more and more, he could feel the oxygen going through his system. He weakly pushed away from the table and sat on the floor as the panic attack left his system. Everything felt weak.

Normally, he would have gone to his mother for assistance with the panic attacks to ask why they were happening. But he had a pretty good idea as to why and he couldn't let her know about the draw. The book hadn't been kidding when it had stated a draw made it difficult for a couple to be apart for any length of time.

He would have to do it. She was safer without him. He gritted his teeth as his lungs started to ache again. He was going to have to find a way to function on his own without going into a panic attack every time he thought of her. It wouldn't do either of them any good.

He couldn't fathom what the purpose of the attacks were, or if they were a nasty magical side effect of the draw. The relaxing elixir had worked, but he couldn't exactly carry it around with him without someone noticing. He pushed himself up to his feet. His legs were still weak, but they would have to do.

He set to work mixing up another batch and considered how to make it more potent. The mix was just a few herbs properly measured together and boiled in water. He stood over the steaming pot and frowned at it. Even the fumes eased the tightness from his chest. He would need to be careful. The warning on the recipe had said it could become addicting if he consumed too much.

Someone knocked on the door. He glanced around for a spot to hide the pot, but it would be useless. So he put the herbs and the elixir recipe book back on the shelf to erase the evidence of what he had just made. Holding his hand over the steaming liquid, he focused on forcing it to cool more quickly and hoped the elixir wouldn't be damaged.

Knock. Knock. Knock. He pulled his hand away to scan the rest of the table.

"Herrick! Open the door," his mother called through

the wood.

It was who he had feared it would be and he knew if he delayed any longer she would be using her own magic to force the magical lock. That would raise her suspicions a little too much. He raised his hand and clenched it to release the lock.

She swung the door open, her eyes narrowed in suspicion. "What have you been doing in here?"

"Hiding." He walked away from the main table to the area of the room full of talismans.

"From what?" She went straight to the table and frowned down at the now cooled elixir.

"You."

She looked up at him in surprise. "Why would you need to hide from me?"

He faked a laugh. "You've been on a bit of a rampage. Have you already forgotten your assault on the keepers?"

She glanced away and her hands clasped behind her back as she went to look at the magical volumes on the other side of the table. "No, I haven't forgotten."

"Have you apologized to them?"

Her narrow-eyed look was back.

He shook his head. "Of course not, mages don't apologize to keepers."

"It's more than that, Herrick. To apologize would be to admit I was in the wrong."

He was surprised to hear her say that she was in the wrong even in a roundabout way.

"A mage can never be wrong in his or her actions to a

non-magic."

Her gaze went to the book which contained the weather spell. He'd closed it, but with a wave of her hand it opened to the last page read. Crap, he'd forgotten to shove it back on the shelf. He had been so focused on his own physical issues. He frowned as he realized the tightness was gone. He still felt a little weak from the last attack, but more like himself.

"What's this?" She was reading the spell and her voice showed it had caught her attention.

"I was thinking about the weather."

She made a humming sound before shaking her head and waving her hand over the book to close it. "Good thought. Too bad no one here is powerful enough without the unicorns to cast it." She leaned against the table and frowned at him. "We should have spent more time trying to find a way to harvest their power."

"The dark creatures killed them to do it." He regretted the words as soon as they were out of his mouth.

She glared. "Are you comparing us to the dark creatures? We protected them from the dark creatures."

"No, I was just stating a fact."

Her glare didn't lessen. "You seem to think it's good the unicorns are out there at the mercy of any dark creature or human. It isn't just the magical beasts who are a threat to the unicorns. People will want their power for their own."

He glanced down at his hands.

"We have protected them for all of these years." His mother insisted. "Cared for them. Our ancestors did not imprison the unicorns when they found this valley. They befriended them. They assisted them. Before the barrier was put up dark creatures and humans frequented the forest to hunt for unicorns. It is because of us this herd has not disappeared into nothingness as so many of them have."

Herrick had learned the Keep history since he could stand at his mother's knee, but he doubted it now. Perhaps the Keep had started out with good intentions, but his mother's own words betrayed what the Keep had become. The unicorns would have no need to run away or escape if they wanted to remain in the valley and have the magical barrier.

The Keep was a prison to the unicorns and they were their jailors.

JILINE JERKED AWAKE, rising to run away from the wyvern in her dream. The tree ring the unicorns had found for them to rest in through the night was the same. No wyvern's raced in or lurked outside. At least that she could see. Darkness surrounded them and she wondered what time it was. Middle of the night or close to dawn?

The unicorns stood in their sleep. Ginger was the only one lying down with her, sharing her body warmth to keep Jiline from getting too cold. The absence of sound told her the rain had stopped outside the magical box. She looked above and wondered if the magical box still surrounded them. She snuggled in closer to Ginger.

A presence jarred her. Her eyes snapped back open.

Had the wyvern's returned? Bai stood beside her. His eyes glinted in the darkness.

She bit her lip to keep from whispering her question.

No. He answered anyway. *A magical search. We felt it before, but what you call our magical box keeps the searcher from seeing us.*

She rose slowly and walked the few feet to bring her alongside his head. "Who is searching?"

The Keep Mage. She has scryed for us several times. His head raised and turned a fraction. *But this is not the same searcher and,* he snorted, *it is not scrying magic.*

"What is it?" She whispered.

Gwyn stepped up beside them. She had been standing on the other side of Ginger a moment ago. *It is your Herrick.*

Jiline shook her head wondering why Gwyn kept saying that. "He's looking for you."

Gwyn touched her muzzle gently to Jiline's arm and her warm breath blew over her hand. *Not us. You.*

She glanced from Bai to Gwyn. "Why would he look for me?"

Perhaps, the Keep Mage has realized she can not find us and is instead focusing on Jiline. Bai suggested.

Gwyn dropped her muzzle again to blow on her hand. *No. He searches for Jiline.*

He is the Keep Mage's son and he is more powerful than she.

Gwyn didn't move from her position, but her attention shifted and Jiline could feel the glare leveled on her son. *Yes, he is. But she would do the search herself. She would not trust another to do it, not even her son. He searches for her on his own.*

"Has he found me?" Jiline looked around the grove. The other unicorns had wakened though they remained quiet. "Does the box keep us safe from his search?"

How had she felt his presence? She hadn't known when Mage Brennah had been searching for them. They didn't answer her and she had the distinct feeling they were speaking to each other without allowing her to listen in on their words.

Bai's white coat glowed as the darkness lightened. She glanced past him to look out at the trees. It wasn't her imagination. At least she knew it wasn't the middle of the night now. Her eyes were drawn back to his glowing coat and her fingers trembled as she raised them to touch its softness. The unicorns had been touching, poking, and prodding her from the beginning, but this was the first time she attempted to touch one of them.

His coat was just as soft as it looked. Softer and silkier than anything she had ever run her fingers against. Dropping her hand, she worried over her sudden boldness. She should have asked to touch him. But he didn't react to her touch.

One by one the unicorns left the grove and Ginger raised up with a groan and a stretch. It was time to move. But the unicorns still hadn't answered her question. Feeling they were still conversing with each other, she walked the few steps to gather her tack. She brushed all the twigs and needles off which had gotten stuck to Ginger while she slept.

Ginger nickered at her and nuzzled her hand. The

pony was hungry.

"I know, girl," she whispered and rubbed between her ears. "They don't give you a lot of time to eat." Her own stomach rumbled reminding her she would run out of food by that evening. "You'll need to eat as they do, on the fly."

She placed her saddle on Ginger and tightened the girth. She then looked at her bridle. It was difficult for Ginger to eat much with the bit in her mouth. Even now there was a blade of grass twisted around the metal. She tightened the girth before tackling the idea of fixing the bridle to not have a bit. The question was how to make it work. The headstall attached to the bit and the reins attached to the bit. She unbuckled the bit and attached the reins to the nose piece connected to the headstall. The funky looking bridle wouldn't offer a lot of control, but it should be enough to direct a well-trained pony. Satisfied it would work, she slipped the tweaked bridle over Ginger's head and put the bit inside her bag.

It is time to leave. Bai said behind her.

She nodded and mounted quickly to follow Gwyn out of the grove. The soft light was steadily growing and though it was still cloudy the rain had indeed stopped, allowing the ground to absorb the water and not be nearly as muddy. The unicorns still hadn't answered her question and she closed her eyes to see if she could feel the presence again. She couldn't.

Turning, she looked at Bai. "Did he find me?"

Yes.

Guilt seized her. "I'm sorry. I didn't know."

Do not worry. It was Gwyn's voice. *He left as soon as he sensed you. He was not looking for us.*

"But he's found you now," she protested.

If he could get through the unicorns' magical barrier to find her it wasn't safe for her to travel with them. She glanced around trying to figure out where they were. Where would she go? Mage Brennah would search for her in her own village. She couldn't go home. But maybe she could go to the city with Madelen and Wilm. But would she be bringing danger to them?

You will remain with us. Gwyn's voice was an order.

"But if he can find you through me."

He was not looking for us. Gwyn's voice was more patient this time. *I know it is difficult for you to understand, but he is fixated on you not us. His concern for your safety was clear in the presence.*

Bai snorted. *He should not have been able to find her so easily. Such is the mind of humans.*

Jiline tried to understand Gwyn's cryptic remark, but the unicorn mare didn't elaborate. Ginger reached down to grab several long stalks of grass growing beside the game trail. She had been right judging by Ginger's satisfied crunching as she walked along, Ginger could eat a lot easier without the bit in her mouth.

HERRICK SAT ON the floor in the middle of his room, still as a statue as his being slid back into his body. He slowly opened his eyes to test that the transfer was complete. A deep breath returned everything to normal. He had found her, and more importantly, he knew where she was. The unicorns were moving quickly for the weather, but since they were manipulating the weather up here it made sense that they would be manipulating the weather off the mountain to their benefit.

The tightness in his chest was almost gone. He could check on Madelen without leaving the Keep physically. Make sure she was all right and safe. Knowing she was with the unicorns eased his mind. The unicorn colt beside her had felt his presence as soon as he'd found her. The warning of the colt had been clear. She was theirs now. They would protect her with their lives.

Confident he could now control the draw and the awful side effect of the panic attacks, he rose to his feet to glance out his window. Yep, the unicorn-infused snowstorm was still going strong. He slid a small vial of the relaxing elixir in his pocket to be safe and let himself out of his room. He was halfway down the main stairs when he met up with his mother.

"Good morning, Mother," he said and bowed his head. He had to be careful not to show the happiness that filled him.

"I was just coming to get you. Come with me." She turned and led him down the hall.

Mage Taika waited beside the table. He bowed his head in respect and waited to see what his mother wanted to attempt now to locate the unicorns. The scrying mirror sat on one side of the table and he considered whether she had been successful in locating the unicorns.

His mother shut the door behind them and walked to the table. "The unicorns still elude me."

He nodded solemnly, but inside chanted yes, yes, yes.

"You gave me an idea."

Well, crap.

"The weather spell you were looking at yesterday to understand what the unicorns had done."

He nodded as if that was why he had looked at the spell.

"I dismissed it when I saw none of us were powerful enough to conduct the spell to the magnitude we would need to disperse the storm and melt the trails until they're passable."

His chest tightened and he breathed slowly from his nose. He would not have a panic attack in front of her. Jiline was safe. As long as she was safe he could control it.

"It didn't occur to me until now that together we might have the power to pull the storm off."

Crap, she had the same thought he originally had. "What do you mean together?"

"We will cast the spell together as one, Mage Taika agrees with me that it can be done. I know you might be nervous to cast a spell of this magnitude."

Oh good, she thought his rolling emotions were nervousness and he nodded.

"But we'll take the bulk of it. You'll just need to follow us."

Could he somehow prevent the spell from working without them realizing it?

His mother smiled and stepped over to pat him on the back. "I know you can do this, Herrick. It'll be a strain, but I have full faith in you."

He tried to smile back, but was pretty sure it was a pathetic one judging by the other pat she gave him.

"It will take me about an hour to set up. Go eat and meditate until then. Bring yourself up to full strength and I'll call you when we're ready."

His body recognized the dismissal and he turned to leave. The door opened and shut for him. He stopped just outside and leaned against the door. He didn't consciously intend to eavesdrop, but something niggled within him.

"He's holding something back from you," Mage Taika said.

"I know. He has since that girl arrived, I didn't understand it at first."

"But now?"

"She must have fooled the other mages into believing she didn't have magic. I think Herrick recognized what she was from the beginning, but she must have done something to him as well."

"Do you think the unicorns sent for her?"

"I don't see how they could, but even if they didn't, they knew they could use her from the beginning."

"We'll need his full assistance for the spell to work."

"Yes."

"What if he holds back?"

"I'll make sure he doesn't," his mother's voice drew closer.

He jerked away from the door and ducked into a keeper hallway just as it opened. She strode past his hiding place to the main staircase. He waited a few minutes before taking the long way around to the kitchen. If she didn't find him in his room meditating, he better be eating instead.

Throughout the hour he thought long and hard on how to hamper the spell with them both suspicious of him. He admitted defeat when he left his room just before the hour was up and found the magical training room locked. That was what his mother had been doing when she'd left her own spell casting room. He went down the stairs, stopping at the base as his chest seized again. Pressing against it, he willed the panic away. He couldn't protect her if an attack came.

"Back off," he whispered under his breath. The pressure eased.

He had to consider what he would do if they were successful in casting the spell. He could protect her physically. The pressure eased a little more. If he convinced his mother he was holding nothing back her suspicions might be eased, giving him just the opportunity he needed to reach Madelen first.

Mage Taika and his mother stood at the table. Candles were lit and unlit. He recognized the configuration immediately considering how long he had stared at the instructions for the spell. He wondered briefly if they worried over the backlash of such a large spell as he had, but kept the concern to himself. He needed to appear to be gung ho.

He smiled confidently when they looked up at him and he strode to the table and looked around like he didn't totally understand what was happening. "What do we do?"

Brennah's shoulders relaxed and she smiled back before dropping into a stern frown. "Follow along with us. This is a very powerful casting. Taika and I will do the heavy lifting, but we'll need your magical support." She glanced briefly at Taika before looking back at him. "We discussed the best way and I think if we put you into a trance that will allow us to draw on your magic."

Well, crap. He had no intention of being unaware of what was going on, but he nodded as he considered an alternative which might suit his mother. "What if you need my help?"

"I don't think we will."

He stepped next to her and scanned the spell in the book. "You sure? It would be more powerful if we all cast it."

Her eyes narrowed. "Yes, it will, but you are inexperienced and could unknowingly cause a problem."

He raised an eyebrow in challenge. "When was the last time I unsuccessfully cast a spell."

"You've never cast a spell this large."

"Neither have you," he hurried to add, "on your own. But you said we would be working together. I know you're worried we won't be able to do it, but I won't let you down."

His mother tapped her fingers on the book. "It would be more powerful if we cast it as three."

Taika shrugged "If he actually casts it, yes."

"Why wouldn't I?" He challenged her.

"As your mother said, you're inexperienced. When you feel the magic well within you, you might back off. You cannot back off."

"I won't."

His mother nodded. "All right, we'll try it with you, but if it doesn't work, we'll put you under a trance to draw on your powers, agreed?"

"Agreed." Disaster averted, he focused on the table and what had been laid out. It was a complicated spell, not just dissipating the storm, but they would have to warm the air to such a degree to melt the snow which had already buried the Keep.

15. VILLAGE

JILINE MUST HAVE been snoozing in her saddle. Because suddenly the herd was stopping and she didn't know why. She glanced around, scanning for any danger. They were on the edge of some woods. The trees had begun to shift from the winter trees which kept their branches year round to the summer trees which were bare in the winter. Rolling hills faced them. There was no more cover for the unicorns to hide in.

Bai stepped alongside Ginger. Jiline was so focused on seeing territory familiar to her own, that she didn't realize the unicorns weren't looking at the grassy hills, but on what was behind them. She glanced back, but couldn't see anything but trees.

Everyone was completely still. She looked at Bai. His shoulder brushed Ginger's neck as he edged closer.

"What's wrong?" she barely whispered.

The mages are striking back.

She peered into the woods waiting for something to come upon them suddenly. But the woods looked as peaceful as they had before.

They have broken the storm.

She frowned not understanding. "What storm?"

The snow storm we called to hide our escape. It has been dissipated. The mages will leave the Keep and hunt for us soon.

Bai turned back and the herd was on the move. No longer walking, but at a slow canter.

She glanced over her shoulder again. "It was Herrick wasn't it?"

Bai gave a unicorn shrug. *My mother says no. I will have to believe she is right. No single mage could have caused the storm to have dispersed. It will be at least a day or more before they will be able to leave the Keep. The air is magically heating around it to melt the snow, but it will still take some time.*

She shivered.

Do not worry. We are far ahead of them. Even if they left today they could not find us that quickly. The box will protect you.

She hunched her shoulders. "I worry for you, not myself."

Which was mostly true. She did occasionally worry over what they would do to her if the mages caught her, but mostly she worried over what would happen to the unicorns. They wouldn't just return. The mages would have to force them. In a battle of magic, how many would be hurt or killed?

None of us. A mage can not challenge a unicorn. They originally imprisoned us through treachery not a challenge. They are not thinking which is not surprising. We hid our escape not for our own protection, but theirs. They can not force us to return to the valley. Fearing for their loss of power they would most likely try and would die trying.

"Then why do we hurry?"

Gwyn's voice drifted in. *For your protection, Jiline. They can not hurt us. But they will kill whoever stands in their way. The Keep Mage will want to punish you for helping us. It is better to avoid a challenge until we can get you to safety.*

Her throat dried at the prospect of Mage Brennah hunting her down. "But where would be safe from her?"

Do not worry. You will be safe with us. Once we reach our woods, no mage can hurt you there.

HERRICK STOOD ON the Keep steps and watched the snow melt before his eyes. Sweat coated him. He wondered if they had gone a little overboard with the high temperature.

His mother stood beside him a small smile on her lips. "We leave at first light."

He nodded. At the rate the snow was melting, the trail would be clear in the middle of the night, but still very treacherous. Better to leave when you could actually see it. Which meant he would leave after first dark.

Her hand touched his arm and he turned to her, worried she had somehow read his thoughts.

"Thank you, son," she said softly. "It might hurt my pride to say it, but Taika and I could not have cast the spell without your full cooperation."

The full cooperation was the most important part of her words and he knew it. She was beginning to trust him again. Good for him as it would make his own escape easier if she wasn't still watching him like a hawk.

He had given everything he had with the spell. It didn't make sense to hold anything back now that his mother would cast the spell with or without his cooperation. That was when he had come up with the plan to leave before his mother would decree it safe. He had to get as many miles between him and them as possible. He knew what direction the unicorns and Madelen had gone in. The trick would be to cover his own tracks so his mother couldn't follow him to find the unicorns and Madelen.

He knew she planned on going around the other side of the valley to try to pick up the unicorns' magical trail. That should buy him some time. He would head directly off the mountain and cut across the grass lands. He still hadn't figured out how he would catch up with the unicorns, but he would be able to find them through Madelen.

Turning, he headed back into the Keep and its relative coolness. It was also unbearably hot, but not as hot as it was outside. Mistress Marta looked wilted from where she waited by the stairs for his mother's orders. He nodded briefly to her before climbing up to his room. Of course, heat rose and each floor was hotter than the next.

He already had his bag mostly packed and he pulled it out from under his bed where he had stowed it after the keepers had returned. He considered each item. He would bring what he needed, but also had to keep the weight down to a minimum. It might be summer and blistering hot up here, but it was winter in the rest of the world.

The rivers would be rising from their forced snow

melt. Treacherous to cross. Normally he wouldn't bring an extra pair of clothes, but a visual of Madelen's own dunking made him shove an extra pair of pants and shirt into his bag. The single cloak would double as a blanket. He shoved in a couple of small spell books which he always brought along with small bundles of the most basic herbs to help in casting a spell.

He didn't know what he would need, but he made sure to include anything related to tracking and protection. A small dagger went in the bag. A longer one he would shove into his boot. He normally didn't rely on weapons, magic being his weapon, but better to be safe than sorry.

Finally packed, he left everything on top of his bed, not worried about concealing it any longer. He headed down to the stables to see what preparations Keeper Brody was doing. He needed to make sure his horse would be ready to go now not in the morning. Eli surprised him when he walked into the stable. He hadn't seen the keeper protector since he had stepped in the path of his mother's magical barbs.

Eli nodded to him, but didn't speak as he groomed one of the horses in the stall. Herrick narrowed his eyes as he passed to reach his own horse. Of course, Eachann was in one of the stalls farthest from the door opening into the snowy meadow. He considered asking Brody to move him, but quickly shoved the words down. Way too suspicious.

Brody stopped grooming a horse when he saw Herrick. "Can I help you, Mage Herrick?"

"I wanted to check on Eachann," Herrick said. "We're

leaving in the morning, you know?"

Brody nodded. "Marta told me. Eli and I are preparing the horses."

The Keep didn't house very many horses during the winter season. About fifteen horses total. There were that many trained keepers within the Keep not even counting the house keepers and trainees. He wondered briefly who his mother would choose to come along. Would she leave Taika to look over the Keep? It would make sense to bring her along unless she worried another mage might try to take it over. Marta couldn't protect it from a mage.

It would be practical to bring along the keeper protectors, but he knew she was still angry at Eli. He glanced at the protector. The unicorns had disappeared on his watch. Did his mother suspect Eli might have been involved? What of the other four keepers within the valley when they escaped?

Eachann sighed with satisfaction at being groomed. Task done, he scratched the gelding under his chin. He would have rather hung out in the stable, but he didn't want his mother wondering what he was up to. Nodding to both keepers, he left the stable to get some food from the kitchen. The cooks were busy and only spared him a glance as they prepared the food the group would take. Lots of hard biscuits and overly cooked meat. He raised an eyebrow at the contraption one of the cooks had designed to try to smoke the meat quickly. Ingenious, but he wasn't sure he would trust the meat not to spoil since it hadn't gone through the normal salting and smoking process.

He picked up an empty food sack and filled it with a canteen, biscuits, dried fruit, and meat he hoped was dried the right way. No one seemed to pay him any mind. He was the Keep Mage's son after all. Suitably prepared, he headed back up to his room to wait for twilight.

THE UNICORN HERD stopped at the crest of the hill.

Jiline. Gwyn called her and she urged her pony forward. *Do you know this village?*

A flash of excitement went through her and she dismounted to crawl up the rest of the hill and look down. Somehow, the lead unicorn was also escaping detection by crouching down onto his stomach and stretching his head out to look over. She hadn't spoken to him before and immediately noticed how sharp his horn was.

She dragged her gaze away from him to look down at the valley below. The village was larger than her own. Fields stretched out all around it and as far south as the eye could see. Dots of people moved about in their evening activities. Darkness came sooner in the winter. The majority of the fields summer and fall crops had been harvested judging by the dark earth, but a few had winter plants blooming.

She shook her head and glanced back at Gwyn who waited with Ginger. She bit her lip and looked around again. Small houses dotted the landscape. If the village was anything like hers, she knew there would be people who didn't live within the village or surrounding fields. There could even be a house behind them. She doubted the unicorns wouldn't have noticed it, but the thought made her nervous. Glancing around them, she crawled back down.

"No, but there could be people in the hills around us and past the village," she whispered.

Our woods are on the other side of the village.

Her spirits raised. "How far?"

Many days.

Her good mood dropped back down. "We should try to keep a wide berth around the village."

That will add time to our journey. A voice she didn't recognize said, stepping up to Gwyn.

She bit her lip. It was up to the unicorns to decide where they went, but she would have thought they would want to avoid being seen by humans. The mages might not know where they were or where they were going at the moment, but all it would take was a single unicorn sighting to have every mage in the land converging on them.

Gwyn lowered her head slightly. *Not a lot of time. It will attract unwanted attention for us to go through the village. Do we want to deal with human hunters following us? A skilled hunter could take one of us down as easily as a dark creature.*

The other unicorn didn't move at first, but then walked to the center of the herd.

"Gwyn?"

We will go around the village.

The herd backtracked a short way before heading north through the rolling hills. They moved more slowly than they had before. And they did travel for what seemed to be over an hour before they started edging west. Trees dotted the landscape over here. Not a forest, but possibly what had once been a small one before the village had been erected and the trees cut down for the buildings. The sun was starting to set when they drew parallel to the village marked by smoke streams rising in the sky. Jiline pulled out her cloak against the chill now that the sun no longer warmed her.

She worried over Wilm and Madelen. Because of what she had done, Madelen's name was ruined. Jiline might be able to disappear, but Madelen and Wilm didn't know what had happened. And Madelen's family. She unconsciously glanced over her shoulder toward the mountains.

Once the snow had melted the mages would come looking for the unicorns and her. How long would it take the mages to discover her hand in their escape? They might have known from the beginning that she helped the unicorns. Would they go to Ainsley right away? Would they do something to Madelen's family? And what of her own if they discovered it was not Madelen, but Jiline who had infiltrated the Keep and freed the unicorns?

She had to find a way to warn Madelen and Wilm first. They were supposed to stay in the city until she contacted them. The unicorns were traveling away from the city as sure as they were traveling away from the mountains. Jiline didn't know exactly where they were, but from the map she had seen at the Keep she was beginning to get a general idea of their location.

She couldn't ask the unicorns to travel down away from the woods calling to them just as she couldn't fathom living with the unicorns for the rest of her natural life.

The herd started to head north again and she spotted smoke against the sky, their course alteration caused by a house on the outskirts of the village. She imagined it would be easy for a single unicorn to move undetected, but an entire herd drew attention.

A dog at the house barked confirming her earlier worry. Not dark yet, the owners could already be in their house, or more likely would be out rushing to finish the evening chores before they lost all light. It was always a race in the winter to see if Mother Nature could move faster than you.

The herd picked up the pace to a trot, but didn't move any farther north. Jiline frowned as she looked in the direction from where the smoke had risen. It was getting darker, making it difficult to see the trail of smoke against the rapidly darkening sky. She glanced at the ground. Rain had come through earlier and the unicorn's tracks were obvious. She frowned considering them and glanced at Bai behind her.

People will assume we are a wild horse herd if they spot it. More rain is on the way to wash our trail.

She glanced up at the clear sky. She hadn't seen a single cloud above them all day or any now blocking the stars.

A shadow moved close to the house. If she could see the shadow, whatever the shadow was could see them.

"Bai," she whispered. "There's something in the trees between the house and us."

I see it. A human child younger than you. We will be beyond her sight soon.

The unicorns put action to Bai's words and they moved into a loose forest, melting into the trees and away from the village. They rode late into the night to put some distance between the village and themselves. The rain blew in just as Jiline dismounted. She braced against the cool wind and untacked Ginger who immediately lay down. She crouched beside her and threaded her fingers through her exhausted pony's mane.

"Sleep now," she whispered in concern.

How much longer could Ginger handle the pace the unicorns set? Bai and Gwyn had touched her several times throughout the day and evening with their horns. But the energy they gave her didn't seem to last.

She will be fine. Gwyn said.

Jiline shook her head. "I'm riding her into the ground. She can't keep going like this."

Bai nickered at Ginger and touched his horn against her ears. *Mother is right. She'll be ready to go in the morning. We rode longer today than before. We will be more careful tomorrow.*

She doubted that. "We could come across more villages, people, or dark creatures, any of which could make us need to travel fast or far."

Bai turned his liquid brown eyes on her. *We will not abandon you, Jiline of Ainsley.*

"You wouldn't be abandoning me. You could travel much faster without the burden of Ginger and I." She bit her lip. Her obligations and guilt weighed heavily on her. "I need to warn my friends and family of what I did."

You cannot return to your village.

"I wouldn't, but I can send them a message. If the village is large enough there will be messenger birds for hire."

Rest now, we will discuss it in the morning. Gwyn's voice was full of disapproval.

She wanted to protest, but didn't. Instead she leaned against Ginger and looked up. The rain was falling steadily. The magical barrier protected them as it had before and she watched as the rain drops evaporated about twenty feet above the forest floor where she lay.

HERRICK SLIPPED OUT of his room in the quiet of the evening. Waiting for the Keep to settle into sleep had nearly driven him into another panic attack, but he had somehow managed to hold it off. Now that he was in motion he could breathe easily. Getting to the stable without being seen was simple. It was inside the stable he worried about. A few mage lights burned. But he didn't see anyone about when he peeked in. Most of the horses slept. A few crunched hay.

Moving silently, he went down to the last stall and smiled at his tack sitting on a stand by the door ready to go. Brody had set up all of the horses which were supposed to go out in the morning in that way. Certainly made it convenient for him.

Eachann turned, roused from his sleep by Herrick opening the stall door. He placed his hand on Eachann's nose to still the nicker. His coat glistened and Herrick tossed the tack on without bothering to brush him. Leaving the stable was going to be more tricky. He just hoped none of the horses raised enough of a racket to attract Brody's attention, wherever he might be.

They left the stable unmolested and he mounted up satisfied with the foot of snow which remained. The evening was humid and sweltering. Just another magical winter at the Keep.

Eachann moved off eagerly sloshing in the snow mud. The trails would get tricky as they went and Herrick relied on Eachann's eyesight to keep them on the trail. He didn't have to worry that Eachann would try to backtrack back to the Keep as the gelding was always happy for a ride.

Herrick had napped throughout the day, preparing for his all night ride. He would have to stop at some point for another power nap for himself and Eachann, but for now he held back the urge to have the gelding go into a trot or canter. He might be able to move through the quickly melting snow, but a wrong step would prove disastrous for both of them.

16. HUNTERS

G WYN WAS STUBBORN. *We cannot allow you to separate from us, Jiline. I understand your concern for your friends and you have my word that the next village we reach we will allow you to stop and send them a warning. But to separate is unthinkable. It is because of us that the mages will hunt for you.*

Jiline crossed her arms and glared at the magnificent unicorn. It was taking everything within her not to meekly agree and do as she was commanded, but who knew when they would come across another village. It could be long past the mages going through her own village. Her parents and Madelen's family would have no warning.

An arrow struck the tree above Gwyn's head. Jiline's jaw dropped and she nearly fell as Bai brushed against her. She grabbed onto Ginger's head as the entire herd bolted away. Gwyn and Bai remained beside her. Bai spun to avoid an arrow. It buzzed just over Jiline's head. Bai's nose shoved her bottom and she flew up and onto Ginger's saddle. The pony bolted.

Gwyn and Bai danced around her. Arrows flew and

she crouched down as fear clawed at her. They could be hit. The herd was already out of sight. But Gwyn and Bai had stayed behind to protect her from... She didn't even know who or what was trying to hit them.

Her thoughts went to the girl child of the village. Could it be people from the village hoping to claim a unicorn horn?

She glanced over her shoulder as five horses burst through the grove they had passed through only moments before. It was humans, not dark creatures, which chased them. She slid her hands along Ginger's neck, urging her pony faster, but she glanced over her shoulder again. Their horses easily outmatched Ginger and it would be moments before the people would draw alongside her.

"You have to leave me," she shouted at Gwyn.

The unicorn mare tossed her head, but didn't lengthen her stride. She neighed and suddenly stopped. Jiline sat up to pull Ginger up, but the pony didn't listen.

Go! Bai ordered her as he spun to face the people with his mother.

No, no, no. She tugged on the reins, but Ginger didn't listen to her. She was being commanded by the unicorns. Jiline looked down at the sweeping grass and kicked her feet from the stirrups.

You will hinder us! Gwyn's voice was clear.

Jiline closed her eyes and obeyed the command. Her feet found the stirrups and she stopped pulling on Ginger and gave the pony her head. Tears built up behind her eyes before breaking free and flowing down her cheeks. She buried her face in Ginger's mane before trying to wipe her eyes clear. Even if Ginger was being commanded by the unicorns, the pony was her responsibility and she needed to make sure they didn't ride into a ditch or a tree.

She glanced over her shoulder, but Ginger had taken them over a hill and was dropping out of sight. Her last glance was of Bai rearing up and Gwyn standing still as the people reached them.

Ginger didn't slow, but continued to race as if they were being pursued long past her natural point of exhaustion. Jiline's back ached from leaning over for so long, but she tried to ease Ginger's burden as much as she could. At last, the unicorn herd came into sight. Ginger slowed to a trot and then stopped, her sides heaving. Jiline threw herself off her pony, her legs shaking, but she wouldn't allow them to buckle as she loosened Ginger's girth and forced the pony to hand walk.

Ginger resisted, but slowly stumble-walked after her. More tears filled her eyes and her chest compressed. Ginger's head dropped down. Her pony had run herself close to death to protect them. A unicorn approached and she closed her eyes. They would blame her for Bai and Gwyn staying behind.

The unicorn brushed his horn along the top of Ginger's mane, and as with Bai and Gwyn, Ginger seemed to rise up an inch. Her breathing slowed and she didn't stumble as she stepped up to Jiline.

"Thank you," she whispered.

Do not concern yourself for the safety of your protectors. The voice was another new one.

She patted Ginger on her neck and didn't look at the unicorn stallion. "They stayed behind to fight them."

A few men cannot hurt them. You saw how they commanded your pony. Do you think those men still have control over their horses?

"The arrows."

Easily avoided.

"But you ran from them," she protested. Why would they run if the men didn't pose a threat?

To avoid a confrontation. We do not kill lightly or eagerly. They angered Gwyn in their pursuit of you. She will not show them mercy.

She looked at the unicorn stallion before glancing back from where they had just come. "They're all right, Gwyn and Bai?"

Of course, they move to rejoin us now. Their wish was to remove you from danger just in case there were more hunters than had revealed themselves.

"Thank you—" she paused not knowing what to call the unicorn stallion.

My name is Bylun, Jiline of Ainsley.

"Thank you, Bylun."

He seemed to nod, but didn't move off as she had expected. He stood near her as she slowly walked Ginger back to a normal recovery. The sweat still coated her, but her breathing had returned to normal.

Bai and Gwyn danced into sight. No fatigue showed in their strides as they rejoined their herd, touching noses as they moved to Jiline. Her gaze skittered over the red on their horns.

Bai didn't pause before tapping his horn to Ginger.

"She's all right now, Bylun helped her," she reassured him.

Bai flicked his ears at Bylun as the stallion moved away from them. *She is bolstered by the magic, but she is still weak.*

She nodded. She had thought as much and she hugged Ginger's neck. Taking advantage of Jiline not walking her, she dropped her head to graze.

We must continue forward. Gwyn said softly. *They might have friends who will come looking for them.*

She was about to ask if any of the men had survived, but she bit her tongue. "Did you ever need the protection of the Keep?"

Gwyn shook her head. *It is a long story, Jiline. We have always been able to defend ourselves. But can a human kill a unicorn? Yes, if a unicorn is caught unaware and is weak from using too much magic or ill, a human could kill a unicorn and gain its horn for a trophy. But that is all they gain. Our magic goes with us when we die.*

Bai paced around Ginger. *You cannot ride her. She is too weak.*

She nodded. The herd was already beginning to move off and she started to walk and lead Ginger. Bai huffed.

You are too slow.

She would have laughed if she wasn't so rung out. "I know. Another reason it would be better for me to go off on my own."

Gwyn's silent disapproval vibrated through her.

You will ride me. Bai said.

She stumbled and spun to look at him in surprise. "I

couldn't."

You will. He danced forward and stood next to her.

She shook her head and stepped back. "I couldn't."

Why not? It was Gwyn's question.

"You're unicorns. It would be...disrespectful."

You respect Ginger yet you ride her. Bai pointed out. *Mother will bolster her, but it will be easier if she doesn't have to carry you. Get on.*

She chewed on her lip, the order was clear in his voice. She took the bridle off Ginger's head and tied it to the saddle slowly trying to delay; afraid to turn and face Bai. She tightened the girth a little, enough so the saddle wouldn't fall, but not the amount needed for a heavy rider shifting their weight.

Bai gracefully kneeled down and Gwyn bumped Jiline closer. She hesitated again, raising her hand above his mane as she would if she were swinging onto one of the plow horses. He turned his head slightly to glare at her, but didn't say anything.

It felt wrong to grip his silky mane in her hand, but she gritted her teeth and swung up the short distance. Astride, he raised back up and shifted his weight as if getting used to the burden of a rider.

Her legs tightened at his quick movements and out of necessity, she gripped his mane with both hands.

This won't work if you dump her. Gwyn scolded.

I'm just getting used to the feel of her.

She glanced up to see the entire herd had stopped and were staring at them. Bai pranced forward, his movement like flowing water. Ginger nickered and trotted forward as well, a spring in her step. Gwyn must have bolstered her while Jiline had been trying to adjust to the mind altering knowledge that she was riding a unicorn.

HERRICK WOKE FROM sleep drenched in sweat, the panic attack closing around him. Madelen was in danger. He was on his feet before he realized he had risen. The sun shone where he stood, but a few yards away it poured rain. It was the end of the mage weather spell.

He leaned down against his thighs and forced air through his lungs while cursing the draw. He couldn't help her if it incapacitated him. Slowly the pressure eased, but the urgency didn't. What if he was too late? The unicorns would attract all sorts of evil to them, both human and beast. Madelen would be caught between them.

The worst of the panic attack over, he kicked dirt on the small fire he had built. There was no snow along the edge of the mountain. The warm weather had completely dried this area out, but a cool breeze blew through the natural storm. Could his mother turn off the weather spell on her own or would it dissipate in time? He looked up considering what they had unleashed, but he didn't have time to worry over that.

Saddling Eachann, he pulled his cloak tight around him and chewed on some smoked meat as he considered his course. They had probably left the Keep by now. And his trail would be clear since he hadn't tried to conceal his way down the mountain. He'd gone the same way he had gone up. The rain would help conceal his trail from now on.

He should have tried to locate her last night, but he'd been too tired and anxious to get as far from the Keep as possible. He would head northwest until he found a chance to work on locating her. He was pretty sure his mother would either head north to the other side of the unicorn valley which meant she would not come down on this side of the mountain or she would go south to the village Madelen was from.

He frowned as Eachann walked forward. He had to consider the possibility that she might split the keepers up and go both ways. But it was out of his hands. He flinched as Eachann stepped into the curtain of rain. The trail was muddy so he directed the gelding onto the firmer grass and trotted forward. He was going to be soaked through before the day was over.

THE UNICORNS MOVED leisurely, she was pretty sure, for Ginger's benefit. Even with the magical bolstering she was receiving it was clear to Jiline that Ginger needed real rest and sleep. The rain drizzled here and there and streaks of sun cut through holes in the clouds. She had more time to think once the shock of actually riding a unicorn had worn off. With Ginger she had been partially occupied with the act of riding and hadn't had much time to worry over her friends and family. But now she watched the scenery go by, taking her farther and farther away from her home, from her friends and family. The unicorns took her safety seriously and wouldn't allow her to leave. She almost smiled as she realized her circumstances had flipped to that of the unicorns' previous predicament.

She was now effectively their prisoner for her own safety as the Keep had claimed to protect the unicorns.

We are protecting you. Bai said.

She jerked guiltily, it was easy to forget they could read her mind at will. "I know you are. I'm just wondering, when we get to your woods, what will I do?"

It was Gwyn who answered her question. *Whatever you choose. You can stay with us if you like or leave. We only wish to take you away from the reach of the mages. They will not only punish you for your part in our escape, but it is very likely they will try to use you to find us if they can.*

"Wouldn't it be better for me not to know where your woods are?"

Gwyn was silent a moment. Bai danced beneath her and she slid her fingers along his silky neck.

I will consider your reasoning.

Jiline blinked in surprise. Gwyn had actually agreed she had a point. "Thank you."

Gwyn went back to pacing alongside Ginger. She brushed her horn against the pony again, but Jiline couldn't see any improvement. She frowned, but didn't get a chance to protest when the herd suddenly stopped.

We will rest here for a little while. Bai knelt down.

She slid carefully off his back, her natural inclination to pat his neck in thanks suppressed.

I don't mind.

She bit her lip. "Mind what?"

You may pet me if you like.

Her cheeks heated and she smoothed her hand down his shoulder. His softness was unlike anything she had ever felt. Ginger groaned as she lowered herself to the ground. Jiline ran over but didn't get the saddle removed in time. She unbuckled the girth so it wasn't binding, but Ginger had already laid down on the saddle making it impossible to get it off unless she raised up.

She crouched down and rubbed Ginger's neck instead as the pony closed her eyes to sleep. A unicorn approached. She glanced up. It was Bylun. He slid the tip of his horn along Ginger's neck.

It will help her body recuperate faster. Speed up the healing process of sleep.

"Thank you," she said, but he was already moving back to the herd.

Jiline sat down next to Ginger, sliding her fingers through her mane as she listened to her pony's steady breathing. The clouds slowly cleared and she could see the sun as it moved to the evening spot in the sky.

She double worried. One that the hunters had friends who would reach them because they rested. And two that Ginger wouldn't survive this journey.

She is strong.

Bai stood over them as the other unicorns spread out to graze. The magical barrier seemed to stretch out forever and she recalled how the valley floor never saw any snow with the unicorns within.

She nodded slowly in response to Bai's comment.

"She's always been plucky. That's what my father said when he bought her. We even thought about calling her Plucky, but she already responded to the name the spice traders had given her."

She held back the question of when they would move off, but was pretty sure Bai knew what she was thinking. He didn't say anything so she laid down in the grass next to Ginger to watch the clouds drift by.

She felt his presence before Bai went immobile as a statue. Gwyn was instantly beside her as well. Bai snorted a warning and the other unicorns raised their heads.

Jiline looked around, but saw nothing. "Gwyn?"

Yes, it is your Herrick. He searches for you.

"I don't see him." The presence she had felt in the woods hadn't been clear then, but it felt solid now.

It is his spirit.

Bylun separated from the herd. *It is time to move.* His horn flashed as his head moved around in a quick dance.

Gwyn watched him unimpressed. *He does not search for us. You cannot block him.*

Bylun glared at her. *She must learn to block him.*

The herd slowly gathered and started their journey again. Ginger raised her head and shook it groggily. The unicorns had probably roused her. Jiline stood up as action set about her, but she could still feel him. She looked at Gwyn in confusion.

Gwyn brushed her muzzle against Jiline's shoulder. *Yes, he is still here. Do not worry, Jiline of Ainsley, he does not search for us.*

"But in finding me, he will find you," she mumbled.

He does not search for you to punish you or locate us.

She glared at the meadow. "Go away!"

Gwyn huffed in laughter. *Prepare Ginger, the herd is moving.*

Turning away from where she felt the presence, she started to tighten the girth.

You should still ride me. Bai said.

She bit back the protest and nodded before securing the saddle just tight enough so it wouldn't slip off. "Good girl." She rubbed Ginger's neck and was glad to see her walk forward without the drag of exhaustion.

Bai was kneeling down and Jiline jumped on as she had before. The presence hovered near her. Bai thrust his horn at it and the presence faded away.

17. ORFEOS

H ERRICK EXPELLED A breath and opened his eyes as his being floated back into his body. He had located her. He stared at Eachann. She was riding a unicorn. The preposterousness of it hit him deep in his stomach. Madelen was riding a unicorn. Not only was she riding one, but from what he had been able to gather the unicorn had commanded it. She'd gone from preparing her pony to ride to mounting the unicorn.

He stretched out his stiff limbs and got up to mount Eachann. The rain had slackened which was why he had decided to try to locate her, but it was picking up again even under the shelter of the heavy tree he had found. The meadows around her had stretched endlessly, but it had given him a general area to search. The trees which had shed their winter leaves combined with those that had kept them were his best clue.

Eachann galloped out of the grove. The weather had not been affected by magic here and the ground was not overly saturated as it had been at the base of the mountain.

Still the roads were muddy so he stuck to the grass as he headed west.

"WHY DOES HE search for me?" Jiline finally uttered the words that had plagued her since night fall. The unicorns had only been concerned about getting away from the presence and once he had vanished they had been satisfied with a small wood an hour past the meadow to rest for the night.

She watched Ginger graze on the edge of the wood. Rested from the afternoon, she was rapidly attempting to fill her stomach. Jiline's own stomach rumbled, distracting her from her question. She had rationed out her food and the unicorns' bolstering had allowed her to go without as much, but she was down to her last few pieces of dried fruit.

She weighed them in her hand. They weren't enough to stave off her hunger, but perhaps she should save them.

Eat. Gwyn scolded. *We shall find some food for you tomorrow.*

Jiline obediently ate the last of the fruit, but didn't lay back down. Her question was still unanswered.

Bai lay beside where she sat, watching over her as he had from the beginning. She drew her gaze away from Ginger to Bai's shining coat.

She guessed the unicorns didn't have any better idea as to why he searched for her than she did. But it continued to bug her when she should have been asleep. Even Ginger had come to lay beside her.

Sleep. Bai's voice was soft.

She rolled over to look at him. He had not laid out flat, but was curled up with his knees bent under his body and his chin resting on the ground. She closed her eyes. Her body was exhausted, but her mind continued to spin and jump over the question of Herrick.

THICK MAGNIFICENT TREES rose over them as the unicorns approached a forest. Jiline wondered if these were the woods when the unicorns halted, but Gwyn shook her head.

This is an evil forest. Dark creatures abound.

She considered the trees in horror. They didn't look quite as magnificent, but more threatening. "What way are we going around?"

Gwyn shook her head. *We must go through the woods.*

Jiline bit her lip to keep from protesting. Her fingers tightened in Bai's mane. He had insisted again that she ride him to let Ginger fully recuperate. Ginger looked as good as she had on their first day, but she didn't argue with him. She had a feeling Bai felt more at ease in his self-appointed job as her protector if she was riding him.

She glanced at her bag on Ginger's saddle and Bai sidestepped so she could reach down and untie it to strap it to her chest. The darts were secure in their case as she tried to figure out how to keep them handy without accidentally pricking herself or the unicorns. Ginger nickered nervously. Bai touched his muzzle to her forehead as the pony sidled closer.

No one could say horses were stupid when it came to danger.

The herd appeared to have coordinated though Jiline had no idea what was going on as they spread farther apart and stepped into the woods. She gripped Bai's mane with one hand and kept her other on the short sword strapped to her waist.

Bai stepped lightly into the woods, his body moved fluidly as he broke into a canter and darted around trees. Ginger followed close behind him with Gwyn bringing up her rear. The woods seemed to stretch out forever. The unicorns didn't make a sound except for an occasional branch cracking beneath their hooves as they traveled.

She had almost relaxed as they moved through and nothing challenged them. But all of a sudden the air was filled with screaming as creatures dropped from the trees above.

Bai trumpeted and increased his pace. His command to duck down clear in her head, she laid as flat as she could, her worry about Ginger increasing as a creature dropped at Bai's side. He flashed past it. But what about Ginger? She turned and sat up. Something hit her back and Jiline fell to the forest floor.

The stink made her wretch as she scrambled away and tried to draw her sword from its sheath.

Something stepped on her back, effectively pinning her. The weight abruptly lifted and unicorn hooves danced past her face. Fear gripped her. Ginger neighed in panic. She forced herself to turn and look as a creature sat on

Ginger's back, a wicked spear in its hand. She recognized the drawing of the orfeo.

Eli had said a single orfeo had broken into the Keep many years ago and had killed several keepers before a poisoned dart had taken it out. The unicorns couldn't use their magic against it so had to rely purely on physical fighting skills.

She pulled the dart case out as she lunged to her feet. Her fingers trembled over the latch and a dart dropped into her hand. A few feet from Ginger, she stopped and tried to block out her pony's panicked neigh. Drawing her hand back as Eli had taught, she breathed out and flung the dart forward. It struck the creature in its leg barely missing Ginger's stomach.

The orfeo pulled the dart out, his black eyes finding hers as he leapt off Ginger to charge. The dart hadn't worked. Spinning, she stumbled over a log and ran as fast as she could right into another orfeo. Dropping down, she avoided his ax and rolled to the left. Keep moving. Eli had drilled it into her. Keep moving until you are ready to strike.

And she certainly wasn't ready to strike. The creatures kept dropping from the trees. The unicorns' neighs rang out with the orfeos' battle cries. Bai was suddenly beside her. He kicked out striking one of the orfeos in pursuit.

Get on!

She reached up for his mane as she ran. His head turned and he thrust her onto his back with his nose before spinning to confront the single attacking orfeo. He didn't rear, but lowered his head and charged. Jiline flattened herself and prepared for the impact.

No impact came. Bai danced to the side in an intricate move to impale his enemy and toss him aside with the same movement. She stared at the downed orfeo. Pulling herself together, she glanced around for Ginger as Bai streaked past other fighting unicorns and orfeos. At last she saw Ginger, flattened out, racing through the woods with a unicorn beside her. It had to be Gwyn.

They cleared the heart of the battle, but didn't slow as they dashed away. Other single unicorns pulled up alongside Bai and then spread out. Jiline lay flat against his neck. Her head turned so she could keep an eye on Ginger. She ran almost as agile as the unicorns around the trees to where the unicorns sensed the dark forest would finally end.

She looked around when she felt Bai's stride slow a fraction. They still cantered, but were no longer charging through the forest. Careful to stay low, she raised up a little and looked behind them. The battle was long gone. She tried to count the flashes of white, wondering if the orfeos had been able to kill any of the unicorns. She gave up counting unsure if she was counting the same unicorns over and over. They had spread out as they had when entering the woods making it difficult to keep track of them.

Bai's focus was on their surroundings and she didn't want to distract him with her questions. She ducked back down and peered forward along his neck. The forest stretched out forever.

HIS PANIC ATTACK slowly eased. Herrick cursed under his
breath as he straightened away from the tree he had braced
himself against when it had hit full force. Worried he was
going to pass out, he'd flung himself from Eachann's
saddle. He looked around and sighed in relief. Eachann was
a few yards away grazing on the thick grass.

He didn't know what had happened to Madelen this
time, but he was getting sick and tired of the draw
incapacitating him. It was tempting to enter a trance again
to make sure she was indeed all right, but the attack itself
had delayed him too much. Making fists and then releasing
them, he walked over to Eachann and mounted up.

The rolling hills looked similar to where she had been
when he had last checked on her, but he knew these types
of hills stretched out for hundreds of miles north and south
and not quite as far east and west but pretty far. The
unicorns were heading west away from the mountains. If
only he knew their destination.

Eachann didn't seem any the worse for wear
considering his owner's unusual behavior. Herrick
considered why the horse hadn't been concerned.
Normally, the gelding was so attuned to his master that all
he had to do was think a command for Eachann to
respond. He urged Eachann into a canter. They rode hard
until the sun had dipped past the horizon.

He rubbed Eachann down before hobbling him and
building a campfire. He was glad the rain seemed to have
ended for now though all the wood he gathered was wet.

Thankfully, fire starting was one of the first spells he had mastered. Holding his hand over the lump of logs, he mouthed the words for the fire spell. The wood cracked as it heated up and hissed. The fire leapt to life. He pulled his hand back and sat down. The heat warmed him, but he kept his cloak on for now.

Sitting cross legged, he opened his saddle bag and pulled out the small mixture of herbs which would help him induce the trance state to release his soul from his corporal body. Shaking out a palm full, he sprinkled the herbs over the flames.

Inhaling the smoke, he closed his eyes and waited. He floated away. Focusing on Madelen, he zoomed away from the meadow and landed a few feet from her.

She was slightly separate from the herd again except for two unicorns which appeared to be her sentries. She lay in the grass next to her sleeping pony. He dragged his gaze away from her to look at the surroundings. He needed to figure out where she was. At least that was the reason he had told himself when deciding to check on her.

A stream bubbled behind them. He frowned at the double stream and looked past it. Taking off back into the air, he floated up until he could see the woods just out of sight. The strip of forest stretched north and south a considerable distance, but was only half a league east to west.

He dropped back down knowing what had caused the panic attack and completely unable to do anything about it. The unicorns had taken her through Orfeo Woods. They were northwest of his location. But he guessed they were traveling exclusively west. Would they continue until they hit the ocean?

He was much farther south of the Orfeo Woods. He would have to travel west until he crossed the area of the woods before heading northwest. He stepped closer to where she slept.

One of the unicorns pivoted to stare at him. They had sensed him last time, but appeared to ignore him. This time they didn't. The one closest to Madelen stepped forward and his horn waved menacingly in the air.

Madelen sat up and also stared in his direction. He had been surprised the first time she had felt him, but now he was sure it was evidence of the draw between them.

She rose to her knees, but wobbled slightly. He floated forward with concern, stopping when the unicorn stepped into his path. In corporal form, he should escape injury, but he wasn't confident the unicorns being magical creatures might know a way around that.

"Why are you here?" Madelen whispered.

His heart ached and he wished he could answer her, but all he could do was watch and observe.

The other unicorn stepped forward to stand over her.

"But why does he follow me? I don't understand," Madelen said more firmly. She shook her head. "Why do you call him that? He isn't mine."

He looked at the unicorn standing next to her, but he was hers and somehow the unicorn knew or felt the draw. Madelen shook her head again and he sighed. But Madelen did not. At least from what he had seen at the Keep, the books didn't seem to dwell on what happened when one mage felt a draw and the other did not, but he was beginning to wonder if it happened more often than it was acknowledged.

He needed to get back to his own body. He had assured himself of her safety and was narrowing their location down, but he was reluctant to leave her. He wished he could speak with her and reassure her. How far west were the unicorns going? Focusing, he sent his being back to his body.

SHE WAS SURPRISED when the herd didn't immediately move off after Herrick's presence faded. But they didn't seem concerned now that he was gone. She fidgeted on her blanket, wanting to break camp. The tree ring no longer felt safe.

You are safe. Bai said.

"He knows where to find me now," she protested.

We are not worried about your Herrick. Gwyn interjected.

She pursed her lips to keep from snapping at the mare that he wasn't her Herrick.

We all need to rest.

"We have. You don't need to stay on our account."

The unicorns were quiet for a moment.

Gwyn stepped closer to her. *Come with me.*

Jiline hesitated a moment before scrambling up and following the unicorn mare through the dozing unicorn herd to another forest ring. She stepped between two smaller trees and stopped in horror.

A unicorn lay in the center of the ring. Her coat was dingy and stained with blood. Two unicorns stood over her and turned to stare at Jiline. For a moment, she wondered if their gaze was accusing.

You are not the only one who needs rest. Gwyn's voice was soft. *Genna needs time to recuperate.*

Jiline took an unconscious step forward, wanting to help the injured unicorn. "I didn't know. She'll be all right?"

Gwyn didn't answer for a few seconds. *We believe so. She suffered several injuries from the orfeos. The poison is working its way through her. Her magic should expel it by tomorrow night. She will be able to travel then.*

"Can I help?" It seemed silly to ask. What could she do that the unicorns weren't already doing?

Gwyn's muzzle brushed her arm. *If you wish to help, you may.*

"What can I do?"

But Gwyn didn't answer her. Cautiously, she walked slowly toward Genna. The two guarding unicorns didn't challenge her and she knelt down next to the unicorn mare. Genna didn't so much as flick an ear to acknowledge her presence. Tears backed up in her eyes. The mare was very ill.

She brushed at some dried blood on Genna's coat. The sight offended her. Unicorns glowed and glistened. They should never look dirty. She rubbed softly, flaking the dirt and blood from the fur. The spot cleaned, she moved on to the mare's mane and slowly began the arduous task of untangling twigs and leaves from the silky strands.

18. JILINE NOT MADELEN

THE OCEAN STRETCHED out below. Jiline couldn't believe how it went on forever to the horizon. The hill where the unicorns had stopped gave a perfect view of the sea though they were still half a day's travel from the coast. The unicorn herd was going slower and stopping more frequently in concession to the still healing Genna.

Despite the slower speed, Bai still insisted she ride him until they reached the unicorns' new home. It was easier for Ginger to keep up with the herd without having to carry Jiline.

It was hard to tell from this distance, but Jiline was fairly certain she could see several villages dotting the coastline. Only one appeared to be bigger than the others and shapes moved out on the ocean just off the largest village.

She watched the boats wondering at their size. She had only seen small boats used for river travel before and these must be massive if she could see them from where she sat on a rock perched on top of the hill.

She dragged her gaze away from the ocean to focus more on her surroundings. The herd was at ease, but she should have been more cautious. There was no sign of human life below the hill or in the brushy shrub dotting the landscape as the hills continued toward the ocean.

So focused on what was in front of her, she didn't notice the herd had drifted some distance away until she heard the sound of a horse galloping. Thinking the herd was starting to move off, she turned and frowned as they stood at attention looking to her left. She spun in that direction and jumped off the rock as a horse galloped up the short hill toward her.

She started to run toward the herd, but she wouldn't reach them in time. How had she not noticed them drifting so far from her? She pulled her sword from its sheath and turned to face the rider. The horse slid to a stop a few feet from her.

"Herrick!" she said in surprise, stepping back and glancing over her shoulder uncertainly.

Gwyn stood the closest. The rest of the herd had gone back to grazing. She glared at Gwyn. Had they stopped so Herrick could catch them?

Better to control the greeting which was coming.

Gwyn turned around and nudged Ginger away who had started to amble toward her.

She glanced back at Herrick and his horse. It appeared to be the same gelding he had ridden so many months ago. Herrick looked the same as she remembered if a little grungy. His chin and cheeks were lined with beard stubble and his eyes held a tiredness that hadn't been there before. He didn't move to dismount.

Jiline stared back. Uncertain of what to do, she took a tiny step back. He hadn't tried to get around her to the unicorns, not that she could have stopped him. He was much bigger and probably a lot better trained at hand to hand combat. But she didn't lower the sword. She didn't understand why he had pursued her.

Now is your chance to find out.

Herrick hadn't made a move. His horse stood tensely, ears pricked, focused on the herd of unicorns, but Herrick's gaze was focused on her.

"Hello Herrick," she broke the silence.

Her words seemed to rouse him and he swung his leg to slide off his horse. She raised her sword slightly at his movement and he walked up to just a few inches from the point of it.

"Hello Madelen," his voice was rougher than she remembered.

And the Madelen thing...she had grown used to being Jiline again. She took a tiny step back. He was within range to disarm her according to Eli's drills. You didn't move close until you were ready to strike. In a stand off, he had taught, always keep some distance between you and your target.

Herrick didn't follow her, but remained where he was. "I'm relieved to see you well."

"You've been seeing me well almost every night."

His head inclined. His gaze finally flowed passed her to

the unicorns. She tensed, but his eyes came back to her and he didn't move. "Your unicorn friends don't like me much."

"You're a mage. You're lucky to be breathing right now."

His lips curved. "You're a mage and don't appear to have any problem in their presence."

"I'm not a mage," she protested.

She glanced over his shoulder wondering how far behind him his mother would be. She didn't understand why the unicorns hadn't run away or act more concerned. But the herd continued to graze.

"I'm alone," he said.

She narrowed her eyes. "Sure you are."

"It's the truth. I defied my mother as much as you did. I'm probably right next to you on her most wanted list. They search for the herd and you."

"If you could find me—"

He held up a hand and shook his head. "I had an advantage my mother did not. The unicorns are hidden from her and from me."

"That's why you've looked for me."

"I would have searched for you whether you were with the unicorns or not. If you had returned to Ainsley, I would have searched for you there."

"Why?" The single word held so much importance.

His gaze skittered away for a moment, before finding hers again. "It's difficult to explain."

"Try."

"When you left, I couldn't not search for you, I had to know you were okay." He shrugged. "It would be hard to explain to someone who isn't a mage."

"You just said I was a mage."

"You said you weren't." He gave her a small smile and ran his hand through his hair. "I tracked you through the connection the draw gave me. I'm not working for my mother. Do you honestly believe your unicorns would allow me here if I was?"

She glanced over her shoulder. The herd remained unconcerned by his presence. She supposed he had a point. It was his feelings toward her which were making her so uncomfortable. He had found her every night through this connection he spoke of. As much as she might want him to go away, it appeared he planned on staying on her trail.

He cleared his throat and she pulled her gaze back to him. "I won't harm them, Madelen, or you. But my mother is searching for them. I can be of assistance in case she does find them."

"Wait here," she demanded and turned to walk the short distance to the herd.

Gwyn raised her head as she approached. She glanced toward the middle of the herd to where Genna lay in the high grass, resting. Her coat had lost its dingy undertone and was beginning to shine again.

Turning her attention back to Gwen, she asked the question which had been nagging at her since Herrick rode up. "Why did you allow him to catch us?"

Why put off what would happen eventually? We do not fear him.

We are close to our new home and don't want him searching for you there.

She looked past the herd toward the sea. "Where?"

Our forest is just past that hill.

Thick woods stretched out north of the fishing village along the coastline as far as she could see.

"It's so close to people," she worried. The sun was beginning to set. Pinks streaked the sky above the ocean and the unicorns' forest.

It calls to us. Our new home. The other reason we waited. We shall make the last leg of our journey under the cover of night.

Jiline nodded. She didn't have to look to feel Herrick's gaze on her. It hadn't left since he joined them. He hadn't approached the herd with her. Self-preservation held him back.

We do not fear him. Gwyn assured her. *His intentions are true.*

"His intentions to do what?" Jiline whispered, glancing over her shoulder at him.

He looked even older with his beard stubble. Somehow that made her more nervous. She wasn't stupid. The kiss back at the Keep had told her his intentions. She wrapped her arms around her middle as her stomach flipped.

Gwyn's eyes were soft as she lowered her head. *To protect you. To care for you.*

"I'm not ready for that."

He will not act on his own desires unless you welcome him.

Gwyn bumped her with her shoulder and guided her

away from the herd and toward Herrick. Herrick rose from sitting on the grass as they approached. His unease with Gwyn being so close bolstered Jiline's own courage.

But Gwyn didn't threaten him in any way. *You must tell him how you feel. He has pledged himself as your protector. You wish to see your friends, your family, we can not help you, but he could.*

Jiline bit her lip. "Herrick," she paused, "I don't have feelings for you."

"I know." His voice was soft and understanding. "I don't expect you to."

The pinks faded to grayness. Gwyn moved away and Ginger trotted up.

It is time to go.

Ginger bumped her nose against Jiline's hand and nickered to Herrick's horse. His horse returned the greeting with a nicker of his own. Ginger preened.

Jiline looked down at the ground. "I don't understand."

He nodded. "I didn't either. The connection we feel is tied to our magic. When you're in danger, I feel it. The farther away you are from me the more my magic demands I find you. The mages call it a draw. A magical connection to another person. Their well-being is more important than anything else. I can't *not* protect you." He glanced away and then back. "There's no condition to my protection."

"Why does everyone think I need to be protected and cared for?"

His lips curved. "You've ticked off an entire legion of mages. They won't forgive and forget. They will eventually come after you. My mother's focus is to find the unicorns right now. How she expects to catch them is beyond me. But sooner rather than later she will focus on you."

His words were true and she trembled at the thought of them coming after her. The unicorns had said as much. That was why they insisted on her joining them in their protected woods. She looked toward the dark shadow where she knew the woods lay. Once the herd moved out, they would reach them within a few hours.

The fishing village below the woods was probably large enough to have messenger pigeons for hire. She could warn her family. Warn Madelen and Wilm of what she had done. They wouldn't be able to return to Ainsley either.

Come. Bai's voice was a command.

She turned away from Herrick to tighten Ginger's girth. Herrick matched her movements and had his horse alongside Ginger as she mounted. She almost smiled at the irritation she felt flowing from Bai. They were closer to the herd than to her, but none of the unicorns made any move to stop Herrick from following.

Nothing would stop him except death. Gwyn said.

Her amusement faded and she looked up at Herrick. Already taller than her, he was even bigger when you added in the size difference between Ginger and his own horse. Ginger stepped eagerly forward, a spring in her step and her neck curved, to follow the unicorns.

"Gwyn says," she hesitated. "Only death could keep you away from me."

He didn't answer her question but posed his own.

"Who's Gwyn?"

"One of the unicorns."

His gaze was steady on hers. "You can speak with them? I wondered how they communicated with you."

"They speak to me, but I have to speak to them as I speak with you. I told you, I'm not a mage."

"I can't speak with them and they have never spoken to me. I would say you're more of a mage than I. You've befriended unicorns. The one creature closest to pure magic than any other."

She shrugged. She was glad for the friendship Bai and Gwyn offered her, but she didn't believe it was more than it was. She had been able to assist them with something they had been wanting to do for a long time and they were grateful to her for her help. Of course, now they felt responsible for her and wouldn't allow her to leave them.

"You didn't answer my question," she said.

He glanced away. "I told you. I can't not protect you."

"Of course you can. You turn your horse and ride back to the Keep."

He made a noise, but she wasn't sure if it could be described as a laugh. "If it was only that simple."

Jiline bit her lip thinking of the draw he described. She didn't understand it, but she remembered the look of misery on Madelen's face over being separated from Wilm for the rest of her life. They hadn't gone to quite the extreme that Herrick had to be with each other, but many people would probably think they had taken it too far for her to defy the mages even if it was Jiline's suggestion.

"Will your mother really come looking for me?"

He nodded. "She wanted to look for you the moment she learned you were gone. Bringing your pony was a nice touch. I was able to plant a seed of doubt on whether you had actually helped the unicorns escape or had rather taken advantage of a situation to run away as the storm started."

"Eli didn't give me away?"

He slowly looked at her. "Eli was involved?"

She bit her lip and nodded just as slowly. "I guess he didn't." She held back the knowledge of him releasing Ginger. "He saw us go through the barrier."

"He saw you?"

She nodded again.

"No, he didn't reveal what he had witnessed. I believe he told my mother he didn't see or hear anything strange. The keepers slowly realized they should have seen a unicorn, but hadn't."

His draw was still the primary thought running through her mind, but she didn't know how to ask him, it felt almost mean considering she didn't feel anything toward him. He rode silently behind her. She glanced over her shoulder and he smiled slightly.

"I still don't understand why you can't leave. Why you feel compelled to...protect me?"

His smile faded. "I know you don't. I don't understand how the unicorns communicate with you, but I believe it to be true because I'm comfortable with the world of magic."

"So, it's like I cast a spell on you."

His small smile returned. "In a way, but not accurate.

You didn't actually cast a spell to link me to you. It's simpler and more complicated than that. The mages believe it's a magical way to recognize who your true...mate should be. I was raised to believe it always occurred between two people, but now I'm starting to wonder if it isn't more frequent for a single mage to feel it while the other doesn't. The books only touched on the possibility." He glanced down at his hands and shrugged. "It's funny what we remember when our view is shifted. I can think of a few mages who this might have happened to."

"Do they follow the person they're attached to around?"

He shook his head. "Not that I know of, but I can remember them coming to the Keep for assistance and being extremely ill when first separated. I didn't know what ailed them at the time, but I wonder if it could be related."

"So you could separate from me?"

His eyes met hers and they were fierce in expression. "No."

"But you just said."

"I regret telling you so much. The Keep is not what it was without the unicorns. Who's going to magically lock me in a room to prevent me from following you? Who's going to keep my body from killing itself as it tries to escape?"

She stared at him caught off guard by the intensity of his words. Was it really that difficult? Didn't he hate being tied to her in such a way? She hated knowing he couldn't leave if he wanted to.

"I just thought you would like your freedom back. Perhaps there are other mages who could help?"

His gaze softened. "How about if I start to grow tired of knowing you're safe that I seek out one of those mages?"

"You don't need to make fun of me."

He shook his head. "My words might have been in jest, but my meaning was not. I have no desire to break the draw if it could be done, but if a time should arise, I'll tell you."

Biting her lip, she nodded. They conducted the rest of the ride in silence until they reached the edge of the magical woods. She didn't know how she knew the woods were magical. But the feeling emanated from them.

"Madelen," Herrick said behind her.

She hunched her shoulders and turned as Herrick let his horse draw alongside Ginger. She had grown used to not being Madelen and it seemed wrong to deceive him considering all he had given up because of his magical induced devotion to her. "My name's Jiline not Madelen."

19. UNICORN FOREST

Herrick raised an eyebrow, flummoxed for a moment. "Jiline?"

She shrugged, her gaze not quite reaching his. "My friend, Madelen, was set to marry when your mages selected her to be a keeper. I traded places with her."

Her explanation was so simple yet explained so much; for instance, how a dormant mage had made it past their paltry safeguards.

The unicorns slowly disappeared into their new woods. Her gaze was focused on them. The two that had claimed her remained, waiting for her to join them. He knew in his heart he wasn't welcome in the woods as she was. He dismounted.

Jiline glanced at him. "What are you doing?"

"I'm not welcome in the woods, Jiline," he said her name to reinforce it in his mind. "I'll make camp here."

She looked around them. "What if someone sees you?"

He shrugged. "Then I'm a traveler making camp just outside these woods." He looked at the village south of them. "I've never traveled this far north up the coast. No one will know who I am."

"And what if I never come out of these woods?" Jiline asked sharply.

"I shall build a little cabin for myself and a corral for Eachann." He didn't look at her as he said it. "Looks like a nice place to grow old."

Ginger stepped closer to him. He hoped it was Jiline directing her pony. Maybe there was a smidgen of caring for him inside her. Even if she didn't recognize it for what it was.

"You'll just stay here for the rest of your life? I'll be safe in the woods. The unicorns told me."

He looked at her then. "I know. But I also know my mother will never stop looking for the unicorns. The number of searchers will go up once word spreads of her losing possession of them."

She still didn't understand that he couldn't physically leave her at this time. He wasn't sure how the draw would be affected by the unicorns' presence. Maybe knowing she was in the woods safe with them would ease the pressure, but at the moment his chest was tightening knowing she would be out of his sight in moments.

The urge to grab onto her was strong, but he shackled it in. Not only would she not welcome his embrace, but he had promised himself he wouldn't force the other part of the draw on her. She was still young. Technically, she was of marrying age, but most girls waited another year or two unless necessity forced a younger marriage.

A small part of him had hoped that once she saw him the draw would be ignited within her. He hoped it had been hidden as her magic has been hidden. But it wasn't. He could feel the magic flowing through her. It was a small stream, but it was there. With practice and age the flow would increase. He had no doubt she would reach mage powers within a couple of years.

How she had accomplished freeing the unicorns was beyond his understanding. The barrier fed off the unicorns' magic – they couldn't direct any of their magic at it without it increasing the barrier strength. His mom had said it was so a mage or non-magic couldn't force a unicorn to break free, but he seriously doubted the reasoning knowing what he knew now.

Jiline hadn't ridden off despite his silence and he turned to her. He might as well ask. "How did you break the barrier? I don't think I could break the barrier and I, no offense, have more power than you."

Her cheeks turned red and he wondered what could embarrass her about his question unless she actually hadn't had anything to do with the barrier breaking. Perhaps a dark creature had broken through and the unicorns had simply taken advantage of the situation.

"You could have broken the barrier," she whispered, glancing over her shoulder at the unicorns waiting patiently for her.

Well, one of them was still, the other tossed its head occasionally.

He didn't answer right away, because his natural

reaction was to disagree with her.

"The unicorns explained to me that you haven't begun to draw on their magic, right?"

He nodded, his eyes tracking to them again. "I wasn't old enough."

"Once you did, you would no longer be able to break the barrier. It would have sensed the unicorn magic within you, but until then the barrier could be...manipulated."

"You manipulated it?"

"Partially." She suddenly dismounted and patted Ginger's neck. Her eyes didn't meet his. "You kissed me in the Keep that night."

"Yes." He was about to apologize, but something held him back as he realized she wasn't accusing him but making a statement.

"Bai said your magic clung to me." Her eyes flickered to his before darting away. She shrugged suddenly. "He directed my magic along with your residual magic to bend the barrier."

His lips twitched as he considered the prospect that he had been integral in the unicorns' escape. "You needed my magic to break the barrier."

To kiss her had been inappropriate in the moment, but the draw had compelled it. He considered the magical quality of the draw and the unicorns being creatures of pure magic. Had he somehow known what she was going to do? He had never heard of a simple kiss causing a magical transference, but that was what she described.

She nodded. "As you said, I'm not very powerful. I

didn't have enough magic to do what needed to be done."

"Don't underrate your abilities, the unicorns wouldn't have chosen you if you couldn't help them."

She finally met his gaze. "Thank you."

"It's true. They certainly didn't choose me." One unicorn was tossing his head more furiously. "I think your unicorns are becoming impatient."

"I know." Her lips curved into a small smile. But her eyes remained on him and he felt like she was finally looking at him for the first time.

The moment seemed to stretch on forever. She broke the gaze and turned to lead Ginger into the woods. She looked back as the unicorns darted in. "Are you sure you want to stay out here?"

No, he would have much rather stayed by her side, but this was as close as he was going to get. The magical no trespassing sign was alive and bright. Since she couldn't sense it he knew the unicorns wanted her with them. "I'll be fine."

JILINE ENTERED THE woods reluctantly. She kept glancing over her shoulder until the trees blocked her view of Herrick. She had been horrified when he had first shown up, but now she was hesitant to leave him. She didn't know where Bai and Gwyn had darted off to.

She stopped and really looked around for the first time. The woods were airy with a mixture of many types of trees. It was unlike any of the forests they had gone through before. It wasn't even similar to the small wood strips within the valley floor. For some reason she had pictured the enchanted woods to be identical to the valley floor. But it was its own living breathing entity.

Birds chirped and small furry creatures darted up and down the trees. She wondered if it was always this busy or if they were just noticing the new arrivals.

At last Gwyn reappeared with Bai and Bylun behind her. They flitted through the woods in a relaxed dance before coming to stand beside Jiline.

"Herrick says he isn't welcome within the woods." She bit her lip surprised by her own words.

Gwyn dropped her head. *He is a mage.*

"But he says I am as well." She couldn't believe she was protesting. "I'm sorry, I don't mean to question you. This is your home."

It is your home as well. Gwyn turned her head slightly toward Bylun. *You may tell Herrick that he may enter. We might not show ourselves to him, but neither will we attack as long as we believe his intentions are true. But we will not extend that courtesy to any mage who has used unicorn magic.*

Jiline nodded eagerly. She was about to turn to go back to him when something stopped her and she looked back at Gwyn. "Why am I so concerned for him?"

You needn't be. Bai said. *He is fine outside the woods.*

Gwyn tossed her head in reproach. *You feel concern for him as he does for you.*

"Are you saying I feel this draw he talked about?"

Only you can determine what you feel.

"Herrick said it was magical. Can't you sense it?"

Bai snorted. *Yes, but she won't tell you.*

She stepped closer to Gwyn. "Please tell me."

There is free will within magic. If you do not wish to have a connection with him you may stop it.

"He said he can't."

He doesn't know how. The mages don't understand magic as well as they think they do. The draw as he described it is not something you need to fear from him.

She thought of how he had described the mages using unicorn magic to make it go away. "Could you make it go away?"

Yes, if he asked me to.

Bai nodded his head. *Go ask him and we will untie his bond to you.*

Gwyn swung her horn at him. *It is their choice not ours.*

Bai snorted again.

Jiline bit her lip and looked at the trees. Even though she couldn't see him, she knew he was on the other side. "It seems unfair to him."

Bai stepped up next to her. *I will go with you.*

Jiline turned, but hesitated. "Perhaps, I should speak with him alone first?"

Bai gave a unicorn shrug, but didn't step back. She led Ginger back out of the woods. Herrick jumped up when he heard her approach. The unicorns hung back respecting her wishes.

"Jiline, what's wrong?"

She shook her head as he paced up to her from where he had laid out his tack and was making a campfire. He would no longer be in the unicorns' bubble of weather protection. Clouds loomed out over the sea blocking the stars.

"A storm's coming," she said in surprise.

"Yes, looks like a big one."

"The unicorns said you may enter the forest if you want. They won't attack you as long as you don't intend on doing any harm to them."

Or you. Bai's voice was firm.

She wondered why Bai so deeply distrusted him while Gwyn appeared to trust him.

"You shouldn't ride out the storm on this bluff." She tossed Ginger's reins over her neck and walked over to help gather up his belongings.

He frowned slightly and plucked his saddle from her arms. "If you insist." He whistled to his horse and they stepped back in within the safety of the trees. "Looks like the storm will hit around dawn."

A large old burned out tree trunk with several new growths formed a ring and she led him inside. The ring was darker than the rest of the forest not allowing much moonlight in. As the clouds rolled in the moonlight would be hidden. Ginger and Eachann stopped just outside the ring.

She bit her lip. He stood quietly behind her. She could hear him set his gear on the ground and she took a deep breath to bolster her courage. She didn't understand her reluctance to speak since she hated the idea of him being forced to follow her around for the rest of his...and her life.

"The draw." She stopped and turned. His expression was expectant. She hugged her arms around her middle. "The unicorns can break it for you if you want." She rushed on. "Of course you do." She started to walk out to ask for Gwyn. She didn't want Bai doing it.

He grabbed her arm to stop her and quickly dropped it. "Say that again."

She closed her eyes and turned back. "They can break the magical tie you feel toward me."

"Why would I want it broken?"

She looked at him in surprise. "So you can be free of me."

"Again, why would I want to be free of you? I admit it was a little inconvenient at first and painful even when you first left, but I can control it for the most part. I have no desire to be separated from you, Jiline."

"But that's your draw speaking," she protested. "I'm going to live in these woods for the rest of my life. Hiding with the unicorns. You can't tell me that's what you want. You travel all the time. One of the keepers told me."

"I traveled all the time to get away from my mother, the Keep Mage," he said quietly. "I liked seeing new places, but that doesn't change what is."

The wind rustled lightly through the trees.

"Why would you want to be tied to me, to this forest, when you could be free?"

He didn't answer right away. "I'm more free in this moment than I have been my entire life. I want to be here, right now, can we leave it at that?"

She drew in a deep breath to keep from protesting again. It was late. She didn't want to argue with him any longer. What she wanted was sleep.

Seeming to take her silence as an affirmative, he moved back to the center of the grove and began to make camp.

HERRICK LEAPT UP, flung his arms out. "Be blinded, be gone!"

The presence vanished in a shock wave.

"What was it?" Jiline whispered. He was beside her in an instant and pulling her to her feet.

"My mother," he paused, "at least I'm pretty sure it was my mother."

The unicorns suddenly appeared in their small ring.

Herrick let go of her arm immediately and dropped to his knees. "I beg for your forgiveness, I should not have used magic within your woods."

Alarmed by his apology and for his safety, she stepped between him and the unicorns. "He was protecting us."

Gwyn's eyes were soft in the morning light. *We know. We are thankful for his quick action. Was it the Keep Mage?*

Herrick slowly rose. "I believe so, mistress."

You may call me Gwyn. Who was she searching for? You or Jiline?

Herrick shook his head. "I don't know. You are blocked from her so it must have been one of us."

It was him. Send him away. Bai's voice was harsh.

Herrick stayed focused on Gwyn and Jiline wondered

if he could hear Bai as well. It appeared the unicorns could speak to whomever they chose whenever they chose.

She will continue to search for each of you. Gwyn swung her head to her son. *Now that we know we can block her presence from the woods.*

Herrick bowed his head. "No disrespect, but she will simply use another mage."

Gwyn stepped forward. *Always speak openly. You are right she will not stop looking and will use any means necessary.*

Jiline swallowed. "Then we should both leave the unicorn woods and travel as far from here as we can." She didn't relish putting herself within reach of the Keep Mage as bait, but she couldn't stay if she would cause them to be discovered.

No! Bai stomped his foot. *He should go alone. The Keep Mage searches for him.*

If that is true, how long before she will begin to search for Jiline. If she finds Herrick, she will have the means to track Jiline.

Bai swung his horn at Herrick. *I thought you believed him to be true to her.*

He is, but he might not be able to prevent her from using his connection to find Jiline.

We break the connection.

Enough. Bylun's words were final.

Jiline bit her lip to keep from interrupting their argument.

If the Keep Mage obtains either of them she will have the means to find our home. Magical connections or not. Bylun said. *He is right in that she will keep searching until she finds us. We must allow her to find us.*

Jiline shook her head in protest.

Herrick's fingers grazed her arm and he leaned over her shoulder to whisper in her ear. "What's going on?"

They weren't sharing the conversation with him. "They want to allow your mother to find them to protect us from her."

"That isn't necessary," Herrick said. "I'll leave and distract her away from you."

Bylun stood still as statue. *You would have to die for her not to find our location from you.*

Jiline stepped between him and Bylun.

Bylun snorted softly. *Do not concern yourself, child. I did not mean I would kill him. I am simply pointing out that it is not a reasonable plan. We need to fool the mages into believing they have found us, but cannot get to us. They will stop their search and focus their efforts elsewhere.*

Herrick's hand went from a soft pressure to more firm. "They want to trick your mother," she whispered.

"How?"

How much did she see? Gwyn asked.

Herrick frowned and focused on the spot the presence had been. "She was here for less than a minute." He looked around the ring. "She hadn't had a chance to see our location or explore."

Are you sure she didn't appear farther away and walk in? Bylun asked.

He hesitated a moment before shaking his head. "She had just arrived. Her connection was unstable. I don't know if she could have drifted away without losing it altogether."

Then we convince her we are somewhere else. Gwyn said. *She will no doubt search for you again. She came in the night. Any reason?*

Herrick shrugged. "I don't know. She didn't use the same spell I did. The connection was wobbly."

Were you asleep when she came?

"Yes, her presence woke me."

The unicorns were silent for a moment. Gwyn spoke again. *Wait here.*

The unicorns danced away. Jiline chewed her lip. Herrick's body was warm against hers. She wasn't sure if she had been the one to move closer or if it was he. She stepped forward into the chilly morning air and turned to him.

"What are they planning?" he asked.

"I don't know." She paced around the grove.

20. ORFEO WOODS

THE UNICORNS RETURNED. Gwyn, Bai, and Bylun and two others. They had come up with a plan. Bai knelt down for Jiline to mount and she did easily. Herrick hesitated when Bylun knelt as well. A private conversation was obviously going on and then quickly Herrick was astride, uncertain of what to hold onto.

Jiline wiggled her hands buried deep in Bai's mane and Herrick did the same. As soon as the humans were secure, five unicorns streaked out of the forest. The rain fell steadily, but the magical weather box stayed over them and kept them dry as they reached the orfeo's forest. The speed in which they reached it showed her just how much her's and Ginger's presence had slowed their travels. The dark woods loomed over them.

Jiline shivered.

We will protect you. Bai reassured her.

She wished she had known where they were going. The unicorns hadn't shared their plan or destination with her. She had left all her gear tied to her saddle on the forest floor. Ginger and Eachann had remained back in the unicorns' enchanted forest. They were too slow for the unicorns' plan.

Herrick didn't look any more thrilled than she was. In fact, he looked angry. She could hear his harsh whisper, but couldn't make out his words. He glanced at her before focusing back on the trees as the unicorns stepped lightly into the evil woods.

It wasn't the same place they had been before. In fact, they entered a clearing with large rocks in the center. She hadn't seen this clearing the first time they had gone through the woods.

You'll need to go to sleep. Bai said softly.

"What?" she whispered, but slid off him as he bid.

Don't worry. I won't allow anything to touch you.

Jiline couldn't help but worry and think of Genna who had been severely injured when they had gone through the orfeo's woods before. Herrick pulled her close to him. She hadn't seen him dismount Bylun. The five unicorns began some sort of dance throughout the clearing and along the edge. She didn't step away from Herrick this time. She welcomed his strong presence to help keep her fear in check.

Their task complete the unicorns moved back within the clearing and Gwyn approached them.

Lie down.

Jiline shared a scared look with Herrick, but did as Gwyn asked.

Sleep.

THE PRESENCE WAS stronger this time. Herrick woke immediately. Gwyn stood by him. Her gentle command stopping the magic from flaring from his finger tips. He lay still and attempted to keep his breathing under control as the presence drifted away. He slid his hand along the ground until his fingers touched Jiline.

His breathing immediately stabilized assured she was all right and safe. Her hand turned and squeezed his. She also was awake. They lay still together as the presence drifted forward and then back. If only he could open his eyes to see what his mother saw.

His mother's confusion was palatable, but not knowing what she was seeing, he wasn't sure exactly what had her more befuddled. Gwyn suddenly moved beside them, her hooves coming down close to Herrick's legs. The presence fled and disappeared.

He sat up and looked around. The clearing was dark from the cloud cover. "Now what?"

We wait. Gwyn said patiently.

Two agonizing, boring days passed. They could hear the orfeos occasionally on the other side of the magical barrier the unicorns had erected around the clearing. The unicorns kept hunger and thirst at bay with magic for themselves and their human charges. His mother returned each night to verify they were still in the same location.

The bright side was that Jiline had grown used to his presence and seemed to want his closeness as much as he did hers. He didn't broach the topic of the draw or attempt any physical contact except for what was necessary. He spent his days helping the unicorns shore up the barrier against the orfeos. Why they were more active in the day was mystifying. But they seemed to wait through the night.

Dawn on the third morning bloomed bright. Herrick's stomach rumbled in protestation. Gwyn touched her horn to his head to fool his body into thinking it wasn't hungry and then touched Jiline's as well.

"How long can they do that?" Herrick asked.

Her hand brushed his arm. "Not much longer. I can still feel a hint of the hunger after she erases it."

A human scream echoed through the woods. He spun, one hand going to his sword, the other shoving Jiline behind him. The unicorns were immobile as statues as they also looked in that direction. Crashing followed. Jiline jumped to the side and picked up a thick stick she had found the day before. She'd complained when they'd first arrived in the meadow about leaving her weapons in the enchanted forest and how stupid she felt.

He had a feeling the unicorns had intended it that way as they didn't want her fighting any more than he did.

Orfeo battle trumpets! His skin itched. Magic was being cast in the woods. He was unsure if it was the orfeos he felt or if his mother had finally arrived.

Bring the barrier down right there! Bylun commanded, his horn pointing at a spot in the magical barrier.

"What!" Herrick shouted over the din.

They approach.

It seemed crazy to him to bring the barrier down when

the orfeos were on a rampage, but he handed his sword to Jiline and raised his hands to concentrate on the pulse of the barrier in that section. Bringing a section of the barrier down was a lot more difficult than bringing the entire thing down. Getting a lock on it, he froze the energy surge and a hole shattered in the barrier.

The unicorns moved then. He grabbed his sword back from Jiline and pulled her behind one of the large stone tables. He'd tried to stay away from them before and had pretended not to know they were used for dark magic purposes when Jiline had asked what the stone tables were. They reeked of sacrifices.

Jiline wrinkled her nose when they got close, but didn't protest their hiding spot.

Horses galloped into the clearing. He was taken aback to see several unicorn keepers astride. They would be no match for the orfeos. His mother was inside the group, the orfeos in pursuit.

Bring it back up!

Surprised by the command, he dropped his sword to the ground. Finding the slivers of the barrier he rebonded them and surged magic back through the pulse. An orfeo made it in. The others were blocked out.

Orfeos were pack hunters. The lone orfeo realized his predicament at once and tried to avoid two charging unicorns. Bylun impaled him easily and flung him outside the barrier.

Jiline pressed Herrick's sword back into his grasping hand. He didn't take his eyes off the group of riders, but he could feel Jiline slink off behind him. Alarm filled him. What was she doing?

The orfeos' battle cries continued to ring out, but the group of riders were silent. His mother was obviously taxed from using her magic to get them through the woods. He wondered how many others she had brought with her.

"Herrick," she called out, but her gaze didn't match her commanding voice.

Her eyes darted from unicorn to unicorn. The unicorns didn't stand together, but had fanned out to surround the riders. Their horns were lowered and they fidgeted and moved as he had never seen before.

Knowing Jiline was behind another rock, he stood up slowly from his hiding spot. "Mother!"

Her questing eyes met his, but didn't hold them for long. "You betrayed me!"

"Yes," he answered simply.

Tell her she invades the unicorn forest. Bylun commanded.

"You have invaded unicorn territory, Mother. They don't look kindly on mages who enter their woods. You know that."

Sweat glistened on her brow. "I only want to protect you. This place is dangerous. You have held off the orfeos for now, but for how long? Do you want to always be fighting?"

We will fight for our freedom. Bylun said.

"They will fight for their freedom, they don't like being in a cage," Herrick relayed. "I've seen them in action, Mother, I don't believe they need our protection from anything but us."

"How can you say that when only five remain?"

Herrick shook his head. "These are the five who chose to face you. The others," he gestured at the woods around them, "remain in their woods."

"I didn't see any in the woods," she said.

"They hide well, don't they?"

"Where is the girl?"

"I'm here." Jiline rose from her own hiding place.

He gritted his teeth at her exposing herself. What the heck was the unicorns' plan?

For her to believe we live amongst the orfeos in these woods. The mages will think twice before trying to capture us here.

His mother was revving up her magic and he flung up a magical barrier between them before she could strike out.

She held it in and glared. "She is the cause of all this! How could you choose her over your own mother?"

"You were the one sending me all over the country hoping I would feel a draw with another mage," he shot back.

The unicorn keepers hadn't moved. Their horses stood with their heads down trying to catch their breath. It occurred to him that bringing keepers through might have seemed the right decision at first, but could be his mother's undoing. The unicorns had always chosen who would be a keeper. Would they choose someone who would go against them in the end?

He raised an eyebrow. "You came alone Mother. Not a wise decision."

"I am not alone." She lifted her chin.

"They belong to the unicorns." He gestured to the seven keepers.

As one, the unicorn keepers looked toward Bylun. Herrick's mother gathered her reins in concern. Her fingers twitched with her other hand, prepared to defend herself.

The keepers will assist her on getting out of the forest and then are released from their duties to return to their lives.

"They aren't going to attack you, Mother," he said, before she could make a preemptive strike. "The unicorns want you alive to tell the other mages that they will no longer be used. Anyone attempting to capture a unicorn will have to deal with the orfeos before they even face the judgment of the unicorns. The keepers will see you safely from these woods and then you will release them from their duties to return home."

She shook her head. Her gaze darted from one unicorn to the next.

"Take their offer," he implored and meant it. She was his mother. For all their conflicts, he loved her and was thankful the unicorns would release her. He didn't want her to die any more than he wanted Jiline to die. "They only want to be left alone."

"Will you return home with me?" she asked softly.

He shook his head. "No."

Her shoulders straightened. "You are turning your back on your heritage."

"I don't see it that way. You don't need the unicorns' magic. I function just fine without it." Which was a bit of a lie considering how often they had been touching their horns to him since they had reached this clearing.

Her fingers twitched and he couldn't guess who would be her intended target. Throwing shock balls had always been a particular talent of hers, probably originally developed as a defense mechanism. He had only seen and felt them when she was very angry.

The keepers around her still hadn't made a move to leave or turn on her. Herrick hoped she wouldn't lash out at them. He had a feeling the unicorns would consider an attack on their keepers an attack on themselves judging by how they cared for Jiline.

"Brennah." He walked away from the rocks and to the open meadow to try to draw her fire. The unicorns didn't seem to like him particularly well and he was used to what the shock balls felt like. "You're my mother. I know you aren't a villain. You were doing your duty in caring for the unicorns and in tracking them down. But they don't need to be cared for. The unicorns are quite capable of caring for themselves outside of the valley. You've verified they're fine and can report back to all the other mages that the unicorns are living and thriving on their own."

His mother laughed harshly. "You really believe the other mages will let it go. That I will escape their judgment. That they won't come looking for the unicorns as soon as they learn of their disappearance."

"You can't control what the other mages will do or make of the situation, but you can control what you do."

Her eyes strayed away from him to Jiline and then

around the clearing. "You do know this is a place of dark magic! Why would you choose this place over the valley?"

Jiline spoke up behind him. "Because they're free here. All they want is to be free."

"No one is free." His mother's voice held icy disdain. "You are not free, I am not free."

21. FREEDOM

J ILINE WAS BEGINNING to doubt whether Herrick would be able to talk his mother into leaving the unicorns alone.

Bai paced behind her. *This is a waste of time.*

It has been only a few minutes. You must give her time to adjust, Bylun said patiently.

How much longer can we last in this meadow with very little food and no water? Jiline certainly can't. We kill the mage and be done with them.

Bylun's head did not turn to acknowledge Bai, but his disapproval radiated across the meadow.

Jiline spoke quickly. "The unicorns' mercy is running out, Mage Brennah." She stepped a little farther away from the stone she had been hiding behind. Herrick's back was pole-straight in front of her. She couldn't imagine going against her own mother in this way and wondered how he was able to do it. "Will you really force your son to watch when they..." She trailed off.

Brennah's glare could have lit her on fire if there had been any magic behind it. Though perhaps there had been. Herrick had erected some sort of magical wall in front of them. She could feel the energy vibrating off it.

"You are nothing but a silly little girl," Brennah seethed. "I don't know what you did to my son to make him turn against me, but trust me when I say that one day the spell you have cast will wear off and he will grow tired of you."

"I've cast no spell," she said softly.

Brennah's gaze moved around the clearing, stopping when it came back to Herrick. "Make no mistake. They will regret leaving the safety of the Keep. I only hope many of them aren't killed before they realize they need us."

Bylun's head lowered just a little. *Gwyn.*

Yes. Gwyn was positioned on the other side of the keepers. Jiline could feel the power they released even from her distance. It washed over the tired horses giving them the energy they would need to escape the forest.

Brennah didn't so much as flinch and Jiline wondered how she couldn't have felt the energy transfer. Her horse perked up right beneath her. She backed him up a step. The keepers appeared to hesitate, but after a moment several turned their horses to ride to the barrier. The orfeos had stopped their battle cries, Jiline realized. She had been so focused on what was going on within the clearing she had completely blocked out what was going on outside the barrier.

Brennah's horse spun and the barrier dropped allowing

her and the keepers to escape the way they had come. Bai was instantly by her side encouraging her to mount. She swung up and glanced back to see Herrick astride Bylun. The unicorns raced from the opposite side of the clearing and back into the dark forest.

She wondered at their quick escape. She had almost been able to hear Mage Brennah's parting thought that this is not the end of it. It had been clear in her eyes. She leaned over to make it easier for Bai to navigate as he flitted through the forest. It wasn't long until they came through on the other side.

The breeze blew the smell of rain. She looked up to see the rain dissolving when it hit the magical barrier. She had forgotten it was storming. The unicorns had controlled the environment of the clearing completely.

Exhaustion was quickly over taking her and the rest of the ride was a blur. She slid off Bai when he stopped in their ring in the enchanted unicorn forest. Her knees barely held her up and she lay down.

Drink, eat! Bai commanded.

He'd conveniently dropped her next to her saddle bags and she obeyed the first command, but since she had run out of food before reaching the forest she couldn't accomplish the second.

Herrick's hand came into her line of vision with a piece of salted meat. Her stomach rumbled and she snatched it from him. Tiredness wiped out manners and she didn't thank him before she ate the entire hunk. The world swirled before her.

SOMETHING SOFT TOUCHED her cheek. She brought her hand up to push it away and touched a horse's muzzle. She jerked up into a sitting position, fear that Brennah and the keepers had found them flooding through her. But it was Ginger. Her pony nickered at her.

Her heart still beating fast she glanced around the ring. Herrick sat on the other side watching her. She stared back for a moment before dropping her eyes. It was still daylight or was it the next day? She wasn't sure how long she had slept. She wasn't tired any longer, but she was hungry. Apparently satisfied with waking her owner, Ginger ambled to the edge of the grove to snack on a bush.

Herrick rose up slowly and walked over to her. He sat down again cross legged and produced a bundle of food. "Eat."

"You sound like Bai," she protested slightly, but she couldn't stop herself from reaching for a few pieces of dried fruit. "Thank you."

He frowned over her selection, but didn't say anything as his eyes raised to meet hers. She chewed slowly, self consciously at being watched so closely.

She swallowed. "What?"

Herrick shook his head. "I'm glad you're all right."

She hesitated. "I'm glad you're all right as well." She bit her lip in hesitation. "And still here."

His lips curved into a smile. "You know I can't leave you." His gaze drifted over the ring. "Though I might have to leave this forest."

She stopped mid-bite. "Why?"

"The unicorns don't welcome me here, Jiline," he explained softly. "I'll never be far away. There's plenty of grassland outside the forest and the fishing village is relatively close."

Her gut clenched and she put the fruit down in her lap unable to eat another bite for fear of throwing up. "But..."

"I don't want to leave you," he said. "I know you're safe here in these woods with the unicorns."

It was her turn to look around. Flashes of white danced in her peripheral vision just outside the ring. "If you wish to return to the Keep, I understand."

He raised an eyebrow and shook his head. "No, you don't. You wouldn't be making such a suggestion if you did."

"I'm just saying." She struggled with the words. "You aren't responsible for me. I don't want you to feel trapped."

He picked up a piece of dried meat from the bundle and took a big bite. He chewed for a moment before answering and she wondered what thoughts he had been taking the time to gather.

"Do you want me to go over the specifics of a draw with you so you can understand why it is impossible for me to leave? Why I have no desire to leave you? I don't feel trapped."

"But it isn't fair to you." How could he want to stay when he knew she didn't feel what he felt?

He leaned forward slightly. "I don't expect reciprocation, Jiline, so you can stop trying to talk me into leaving."

How had he known what she was thinking while also getting her intent so wrong? She considered her next words carefully. "I'm going to take you at your word, Herrick."

She paused and was able to resume eating her dried fruit. She was sick and tired of rations. She wondered if the fishing village just south of the woods had a restaurant. Or more importantly, a messenger pigeon service, she really needed to get word to her family and to Wilm and Madelen.

Mage Brennah had not given up. She had strategically backed down. She peeked at Herrick out of the corner of her eye. "About Mage Brennah—"

"Don't worry, the unicorns have blocked us from her prying eyes as long as we stay within the forest."

She needed to send off her warnings. "What if I need to go to the village?"

"I'll block her."

"Can you do that?"

He nodded. "The unicorn, Bylun, told me how. I can teach the technique to you in case I'm not with you."

She smiled. "I thought you always had to be with me."

"I'd prefer to be, but I can control the draw as long as you're safe. That way I won't push the unicorns' hospitality too far."

She frowned wondering what the unicorns had said. Obviously he had been up for a little while if they had spoken with him and taught him a spell.

Gwyn's voice flowed through her head. *We will always extend our protection to you. But your Herrick is still a mage. Bylun has convinced the others to tolerate him because of his assistance to us, but they are not comfortable with a mage who has the knowledge to manipulate our magic living within our woods. Herrick understands.*

"But he's not going to do anything to them," Jiline protested. "Where is he supposed to go?"

Herrick smiled and shook his head. "I told you, but you weren't listening."

"The village?"

"A possibility for a little while. It's a little farther away than I would prefer."

Her gut clenched again and she rubbed her stomach. "Herrick?"

He nodded for her to continue.

"This draw you feel, do you feel it in your stomach?"

His eyes were thoughtful as he looked at her for a moment. "In the beginning, now I feel it in my heart."

She rubbed her stomach again. "I don't like the idea of being separated from you, but I'm afraid to leave the forest. What if I lead Mage Brennah right to them?"

Do not worry over us. Gwyn said. *You are always welcome within our woods, but you're not a prisoner. We only wish for your safety and happiness.*

Herrick was smiling again, he slowly reached for her hand and held it within his. "You won't. I'll teach you how to be invisible to her."

"I don't have your abilities," she said doubtfully.

"They're inside you, waiting to emerge. It will take a little time. Until then I can protect you, if you'll allow me?"

"I didn't think I had a choice."

His smile wavered, but he didn't release her hand. "The unicorns are more than happy to protect you if you'd prefer."

"But why do I have to be protected?"

He sighed. "Because you're important to all of us, but it won't be long before you can protect yourself. You're young, only fifteen. Your powers have just begun to blossom. A few years from now and you'll probably be able to out mage me."

She mock frowned. "You know you aren't that much older than me."

His smile returned full force. "Two years older is a lot when you consider the growth of magic during that time."

She ducked her eyes for a moment before glancing back up. He hadn't confirmed that what she was feeling was this draw when she thought of him leaving.

There is a magical connection between the two of you. It grows stronger. Bai interjected and judging by his tone he wasn't happy about it.

She looked over Herrick's shoulder to where Bai stood just outside the grove. Bringing her gaze back to Herrick, she contemplated her next move. He was handsome. The beard stubble he had before was gone now, making him look his age. The stubble had thrown her off before. She rose up on her knees.

His dark brown eyes were questioning, but he still smiled at her. The movement brought her a little closer and she hesitated over what she was about to do. She had never kissed a boy before. Been kissed, yes, but initiate one, no.

His smile slowly dropped as she rested a hand on his shoulder and leaned forward. His fingers slid along her cheek in a caress as she closed her eyes to press her lips to his.

Her stomach clenched in a different way than it had before. His lips were soft and warm. Embarrassment suddenly flooded her and she pulled back. His hand rested at the back of her neck only allowing her a few inches before she had to open her eyes.

His eyes were warm on her and his hand released her as she drew away. She couldn't hold his gaze. Tucking her hair behind her ear, she rocked back onto her heels. She waited for him to say something, anything, but he didn't. She finally dragged her gaze back to his. His expression was neutral. No frown, but not quite a smile.

"I'm not going to pressure you, Jiline, I know you're conflicted."

She breathed out quickly to say the words. "I have feelings for you."

"I know and that makes me happy, but we go at your pace. No pressure. We can start by being friends."

Her stomach relaxed a little with a flutter. She nodded. "Friends is good. You'll teach me to understand this draw."

His smile returned. "As much as I know. I pilfered a few small volumes from the teaching room. You might as well learn some spells as well."

AS THEY HEADED down to the fishing village, Jiline was a bundle of nerves. She kept expecting Mage Brennah to reappear any moment. But nothing seemed particularly dangerous in the bustling village. People barely noticed the two riders who stopped at the messenger pigeons. She sent one off to her family in Ainsley, warning them and telling them to warn Madelen's family. The second she sent to Wilm's place of apprenticeship. She just hoped he was still there.

Duty done, some of her guilt lifted. Not all of it, but enough that she knew she had done what she could to prepare them should Mage Brennah decide to visit. She walked to the waterfront. The ocean drew her. But the young man standing on a rock drew her more.

Herrick turned and smiled, offering her his hand. She took it and hopped from the pathway to the large rock the waves crashed against. The ocean stretched out forever and seemed mad with the storm. They had timed their visit perfectly to coincide with a small break in the storm, but more heavy rain approached.

Suddenly the clouds let loose, drenching them. Herrick laughed and they both jumped back to the path. Her feet stepped lightly as she tugged the hood of her cloak up over her head. She smiled and glanced up into the rain for a moment to feel the drops splash on her face.

"Jiline?"

She turned her smile to Herrick.

"Find somewhere to wait out the storm or head back to the forest?"

She took his hand, her heart light and unburdened. "Or we could stand in the rain?"

He rolled his eyes and pulled her toward the small marketplace where others were seeking shelter. She laughed for the first time in a long while.

ABOUT THE AUTHOR

Angelia Almos formed a lifelong passion for horses at the age of five when she talked her parents into riding lessons. Horses often play a prominent role in many of her books. She writes young adult fantasy, space opera, and horsey nonfiction. She lives in the Sierra Nevada Mountains with her husband, two daughters, two cats, two horses, and a dog. Connect with Angelia at www.angeliaalmos.com.

MORE BOOKS BY ANGELIA

ENCOUNTER AT SHALANA

Space pirate Captain Kristy Ryan grew up the only daughter of a notorious privateer in the Border Planet Region. She learned her trade the hard way - there were no free rides on her father's ship.

Now, she has her own ship, the *Unicorn*, and successfully works in the shadows, the fringes of legitimate trade. Her life is just how she wants it even on those days when her pilot and lover, Andrew Bennet, drives her crazy.

But an unexpected visit from the Military Space Alliance changes everything. Her father disappeared while working a dangerous mission for the MSA. Now, she's being blackmailed into finishing his mission.

HORSE CHARMER

A gifted princess.
A special horse.
A quest for the truth.

At sixteen years old, Cassia would rather spend her days in the royal stables than in the royal court. But as the eldest child of King Robet and Queen Sarahann she obediently performs her duties as the Princess of Karah.

Her safe world changes forever when her father is murdered in the neighboring kingdom of Vespera. Cassia grapples with his loss as her mother prepares her for her new role as queen. Her first task - she must travel to Vespera to marry a prince she barely knows to fulfill the treaty her father signed just before his death.

Nothing is as simple as it seems with political intrigues and unusual powers shadowing Cassia on her search to find out who killed her father and why.

HORSE SCHOOLS: THE INTERNATIONAL GUIDE TO UNIVERSITIES, COLLEGES, PREPARATORY AND SECONDARY SCHOOLS, AND SPECIALTY EQUINE PROGRAMS 4TH EDITION (NONFICTION)

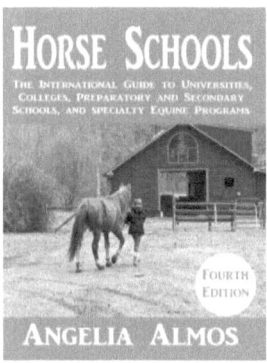

Revised and updated, this indispensable guide features more than 580 universities, colleges, preparatory and secondary schools, and specialty programs in thirty-one countries throughout the world that specialize in equine studies. It is the best source of information available for parents of horse-crazy children, college-bound equestrians, and students desiring a career with horses.

* A self quiz to help the prospective student decide what school is most appropriate
* List of possible equestrian careers
* Icons that show a school's areas of specialization
* School profiles include email addresses, web sites, degrees and majors offered, description of their programs, tuition and horse-related expenses, facility summaries, and opportunities to compete
* A list of equine-oriented scholarships
* Descriptions and a list of intercollegiate and interscholastic equestrian associations around the world
* Multiple ways to locate individual school entries

www.ingramcontent.com/pod-product-compliance
Lightning Source LLC
Chambersburg PA
CBHW032027240626
47154CB00003B/820